Marnie Stevens
Couldn't Believe Her Ears!

"It's dinnertime and you're supposed to fix it," Damon told her calmly.

Marnie's eyes widened. "That's news to me. Since when did you hire me as the cook, Mr. Wilson?"

"We take turns cooking and cleaning up," he informed her curtly. "We drew straws and you won."

Anger coursed through her. "Are you sure this isn't a way for you to get me to do all the cooking and cleaning for this expedition? After all, I'm just a female and hardly good for anything else."

Damon seized her arm, his fingers pressing into her flesh. "Women are good for more than cooking and cleaning. Share my cabin and I'll teach you what else—that is, if you can learn."

MARGARET RIPY

says that the support and encouragement of her fellow writers have been the most important influences on her work. She lives in Tulsa, Oklahoma, with her husband and son and writes both Silhouette Romances and Silhouette Special Editi day, "if only for a

Dear Reader:

I'd like to take this opportunity to thank you for all your support and encouragement of Silhouette Romances.

Many of you write in regularly, telling us what you like best about Silhouette, which authors are your favorites. This is a tremendous help to us as we strive to publish the best contemporary romances possible.

All the romances from Silhouette Books are for you, so enjoy this book and the many stories to come. I hope you'll continue to share your thoughts with us, and invite you to write to us at the address below:

Karen Solem
Editor-in-Chief
Silhouette Books
P.O. Box 769
New York, N.Y. 10019

MARGARET RIPY
A Treasure of Love

Silhouette Romance
Published by Silhouette Books New York
America's Publisher of Contemporary Romance

Other Silhouette Books by Margaret Ripy

A Second Chance on Love
The Flaming Tree

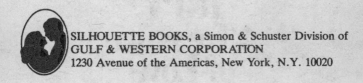

SILHOUETTE BOOKS, a Simon & Schuster Division of
GULF & WESTERN CORPORATION
1230 Avenue of the Americas, New York, N.Y. 10020

Copyright © 1982 by Margaret Ripy

Distributed by Pocket Books

ISBN: 0-671-57170-2

First Silhouette Books printing August, 1982

10 9 8 7 6 5 4 3 2 1

Map by Tony Ferrara

To Helen and Patti
for their help and support

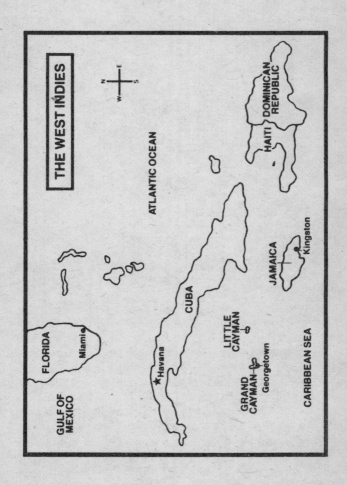

THE WEST INDIES

ATLANTIC OCEAN

GULF OF MEXICO

FLORIDA
Miami

★ Havana

CUBA

LITTLE CAYMAN

GRAND CAYMAN
Georgetown

CARIBBEAN SEA

JAMAICA
Kingston

HAITI

DOMINICAN REPUBLIC

Chapter One

Marnie stared at the older woman sitting across from her in the booth at the restaurant. "Underwater photography!"

The woman waved her hand in the air. "Well, not exactly. Most of the work will be done on land. You won't be underwater all that much."

"Carolyn, I haven't been scuba diving in years! I'm not sure I remember all the techniques." Marnie brushed back a strand of blond hair that fell forward over her shoulder, then took a sip of her iced tea.

"Marnie Stevens, this is your chance to make it big as a photographer. Are you going to turn it down because of one little problem?"

A soft laugh rolled from Marnie's throat. "Problem! This Damon Wilson would say it was more than a *little* problem. He won't want to baby-sit me while I'm supposed to be photographing his treasures." She shook her head. "I think I'd better . . ."

"Now listen to me, Marnie. I fought hard at our agency to get this assignment for you. Mr. Morrison didn't want you to have it, but I convinced him you could handle it. And you can!"

"But still, the last time I wore an air tank was when I was sixteen and living in Florida. That was seven years ago!"

As Carolyn signaled for the waiter, her mouth set in a tight line, she said, "It will come back in no time. It's like riding a bicycle. You don't forget. The first time you put on that equipment you'll remember everything. Now, we'd better hurry if we're going to meet with Mr. Wilson and Mr. Morrison at the office."

"You didn't say anything about meeting him now. I think I'd better go to the ladies' lounge and freshen up."

Carolyn glanced at Marnie as she rose and said, "You look fine."

"No. If this is as important an assignment as you say it can be for me, I must look my best."

"With this book under your belt, Marnie, you'll have enough money to start that project about the Southwest Indian tribes that you've wanted to do. Any editor will be eager to look at your work after this is done. This is your big break, that's for sure."

"I'll meet you at the elevator then in five minutes."

In the ladies' lounge Marnie sat before the big mirror and stared at herself. Large dark eyes fringed in thick black lashes stared back at her.

Marnie frowned as she remembered Anita's striking beauty, so poised and elegant. *Was that why Robert took one look at her and forgot that I existed?* Her frown deepened as she took her brush out of her purse and with long, even strokes ran it through her blond hair.

"Whatever the reason, he's gone, and you, Marnie,

aren't ever going to measure up to your glamorous stepsister," she whispered to herself.

Marnie thrust the brush back into her purse and snapped it closed. Her dress of pale blue cotton felt cool to the touch, contrasting with her smoothly tanned skin. She rose to examine the back of her dress to make sure her slip didn't show. Satisfied she looked her best, she faced the mirror again.

The straight dress clung to her petite frame, accenting her well-developed body. Marnie flipped her hair behind her shoulders, pleased at the simple lines of the dress. *Carolyn's right,* she thought, and walked toward the door. *This job will be important to my career—if I get it.*

On the ride to the tenth floor Marnie moved closer to Carolyn in the crowded elevator and whispered, "What's this Damon Wilson like? I've never read any of his books. I suppose I should buy one and see what kind of writer I'm going to work for."

"He's hard to describe, Marnie. I think I'll let you form your own conclusions about the man. He's the boss man's client, not mine. I've only heard stories about him." Carolyn's features clouded with a frown.

Marnie looked at her agent for a brief moment. *What stories?* she wondered. The door opened and Carolyn stepped forward. Marnie tugged on Carolyn's arm as they moved off the elevator.

"Carolyn, I get the feeling you're hiding some . . ."

Her agent looked at her watch and interrupted, "We haven't the time now, Marnie, to discuss your new employer's virtues. We're late and I wouldn't want to keep *that man* waiting." Carolyn hurried toward the double doors that had MORRISON AGENCY printed in bold black letters on the outside.

Drawing in a deep, calming breath, Marnie followed her agent into the reception room.

As Carolyn approached the secretary's desk, gesturing toward the doors to the inner office, she asked, "Are they waiting for us, Susan?"

"Yes, Miss Smith. Go right in. Mr. Wilson has been here for about ten minutes."

Marnie was disturbed at Carolyn's quick intake of breath. Banishing the feeling, Marnie squared her shoulders and entered Mr. Morrison's office.

When Marnie caught sight of Damon Wilson standing by the large window behind Mr. Morrison's desk, her movements froze for an instant. Then he slowly turned to acknowledge their presence with a cool smile and Marnie began to walk forward again. She felt the full force of the man, the raw savagery just beneath the surface. She found herself standing a few feet from him, taking in his black hair that fell in soft curls, his steel gray eyes, his firm jawline, and the sensual curve of his mouth. He towered a good foot over her with broad shoulders and narrow hips—not an ounce of fat on him.

When Damon Wilson extended his hand to Marnie, she stared at it for a brief moment before she placed her hand within his and felt his long, slender fingers curl around hers. Marnie was drawn to the slate-gray eyes that held a touch of amusement in them. As he released his grasp, she lowered her gaze, a slow wave of warmth spreading over her cheeks. She brushed her hair back from her face, feeling the heat of the blush beneath her fingertips.

"I had my doubts, Miss Stevens, about you going on this salvage until Bert showed me some of your photographs. You're good. I think you'll do justice to my book." Damon picked up some of her recent work from Mr. Morrison's desk.

Marnie thought she heard lingering skepticism underlining the deep, rich tone of his voice and knew Damon Wilson wasn't totally convinced she was right for the job.

"Thank you, Mr. Wilson. I am good and you won't be disappointed in my work."

Damon flipped through the stack of photographs, his eyes narrow, intense. Her breath was trapped in her lungs as she waited for his opinion of the photographs.

He glanced up from the photographs and said, "I don't see, though, any underwater pictures. Do you scuba dive, Miss Stevens?"

Marnie's arms were rigid at her sides and she swallowed hard to coat her suddenly dry throat. *I need this job. I know I can do it,* she thought, then she said aloud, "Yes."

"Good. I'll want some underwater shots as well. But we can talk about this over dinner tonight. Is this still your address?" He pointed to the stamped information on the back of a photograph.

She nodded.

"I'll pick you up at eight o'clock." Without waiting for her answer, Damon walked toward the door and placed his hand on the knob.

Marnie felt overwhelmed by him, an uneasy feeling settling over her as she stared at him, a frown on her face.

Damon looked over his shoulder and added, "Bert, will you draw up the necessary papers for Miss Stevens to sign?"

"Yes, Damon."

"Till eight then, Miss Stevens. Good day." Damon left the office. The air was no longer charged with his forcefulness.

Marnie took in a deep breath and released it slowly, very aware of the masculine scent that lingered in the air. Her flesh still tingled where Damon's penetrating gaze had swept over her once more before leaving the room. Rubbing her arms, she turned to Carolyn.

"I'll have your contract ready to sign tomorrow. Come to my office at eleven. Then we can go to lunch," Carolyn said.

Marnie looked from her agent to Mr. Morrison, who sat quietly behind his desk thumbing his chin. Smiling at the older man, she said, "Thank you for giving me this opportunity, Mr. Morrison."

Morrison's expression remained neutral as he said in a gravelly voice, "Just don't let this agency down, Miss Stevens. Damon Wilson is our biggest client. Carolyn has nothing but praise for your work and I trust her word." He placed his hands on his desk and leaned forward. "But frankly, Miss Stevens, I don't understand why he agreed to take you on. He wasn't that pleased when I told him the photographer was a woman." He made a gesture with his hand, dismissing them with, "Oh, well, he's a strange man. Good day, Carolyn, Miss Stevens." Then he bent his head to study some papers on his desk.

Outside in the corridor, Marnie leaned against the wall for support, her legs weak. She clasped her trembling hands together and sighed. "Well, at least I got the job."

"Don't forget your dinner date with Mr. Wilson and our appointment tomorrow at eleven," Carolyn said as she hurried down the hall toward her own office.

"How could I?" Marnie called after her agent. *How could I?* she repeated to herself, *when I'm not given much choice in the matter. For some reason I feel it could be dangerous to be alone with Damon Wilson.* She shivered and pushed herself from the wall, making her way to the elevator.

* * *

12

Marnie slipped into the cocktail dress. The silken material felt good next to her skin. She smoothed the dress into place, her tanned skin blending with the rich black of the dress. The low neckline just covered her full breasts and the slit in the front of the dress exposed her long, slender legs.

When Marnie walked into the living room, she glanced at the clock on the mantel. *Nearly eight,* she thought. *He'll be here soon.* And when she turned to inspect the room, she heard a knock at the door as the clock chimed eight times.

She looked at the door and smiled. "On time. Somehow I knew he would be," she whispered, and headed for the front door.

When she peered through the peephole and saw Damon Wilson, she threw back the dead bolt and opened the door.

He smiled, showing a row of even white teeth. "I'm glad you're on time. I don't like to be kept waiting."

She stared at him. His gray silk suit matched the color of his eyes. *He's so handsome,* she thought, and again she sensed the aura of power that emanated from him. Words dried in her throat as an electrified silence grew between them.

Damon arched a brow. "May I come in?"

"Oh," she said, and stepped aside to allow him into her apartment.

When he turned to face her in the center of the living room, they looked at each other for a long moment. Automatically Marnie found herself moving forward until she stood just in front of him. She dropped her gaze to the diamond stick pin in his tie.

"Would you care for a drink before we leave?" she asked finally, the spell that bound her to him broken by her words.

"That sounds good." Looking around the room, he continued, "And that chair looks comfortable. I haven't had two seconds today to call my own. That seems to be the way it is when I come to New York. Always busy with the details of my next book." He sank into the softness of the lounge chair and watched her walk to the kitchen. She felt his gaze move with her, pinpricks rising on her flesh.

"I know what you mean. New York is such an exciting, bustling city. I felt that the first day I arrived here." Marnie took a glass from the cabinet. "What would you like to drink? I have Scotch, red wine, and rum."

"Scotch on the rocks sounds fine to me," he called from the living room.

When Marnie reentered the living room he was looking through a pile of photographs. She handed him his drink and sat on the sofa.

Taking a sip, he said, "You are good. I like these photographs even better than the ones I saw in Bert's office."

"I took those last summer on my vacation in the Southwest. One day I'm going to put them into a book on the Indian tribes of that area." She leaned back and relaxed.

He put the unfinished drink on the table. "That hit the spot. I was a bit thirsty, but we must be going. I have a reservation for eight thirty at The Four Seasons." Rising, he began to walk toward the front door.

Marnie hesitated. *The Four Seasons! Anita's favorite place. What if I run into her and Robert?* she asked herself, a surge of apprehension spreading through her. *What will I say to them?*

As Damon turned back, Marnie lifted her gaze to the question in his. She shrugged and thought, *I can't avoid my stepsister forever.*

When they emerged from the building, a chauffeur stood by a black limousine and opened the back door for them, and Marnie slid across the seat to the other side. All the way to the restaurant they sat in silence. Marnie's nerves felt raw as she stared at the passing buildings, her mind slipping back into the past.

Marnie's memory filled with the picture of Anita clasped in Robert's arms in Marnie's apartment the day she had returned early. Marnie again felt the hurt and bitterness as she visualized Robert scrambling to his feet, a look of anger on his face. Then Marnie remembered looking at Anita and seeing her stepsister's features shrouded with desire. She could remember turning and fleeing the apartment, only to return later and find all of Anita's things gone. A shudder worked its way through her when she thought of finding the note Anita had written her. Imagining the words again, she went over them in her mind. Marnie would never forget the despair she had felt when she had read that her stepsister had moved in with Robert.

Marnie clamped her jaws together, blocking from her mind the bitter memories and concentrating on the man sitting next to her. For the first time she noticed that his thigh pressed into hers. She smelled his cologne; she sensed his leashed control. He reminded her of a leopard as it waited to strike its prey, and she inched closer to the window.

When the limousine halted in front of the restaurant, Marnie drew in a relieved breath. Damon helped her from the limo, the cool breeze of evening fanning her heated cheeks. The two of them moved into the dimly lit restaurant with its chic contemporary decor.

After the headwaiter showed them to their table and handed them their menus, Marnie surveyed the large room. She wanted her stepsister to see her with this handsome man and yet, at the same time, she dreaded seeing Anita. Marnie's stomach twisted into a knot of nerves.

She studied each couple, the knot loosening as she assured herself that Anita wasn't there. A small gasp escaped her lips when Damon spoke, cutting into her thoughts and bringing her back to the man across from her.

"What would you like to order?" he asked.

"I'll have the Boeuf à la Ficelle," Marnie answered.

When the waiter placed the Boeuf à la Ficelle with Sauce Moutarde Bâtarde in front of her, Marnie looked at Damon. "I'm hungry but I don't think I'll be able to finish all of this. This was meant for two people."

He laughed. "Eat what you can." The laugh lines at the corners of his eyes deepened. "You aren't one of those women who's continuously dieting, are you?"

"No, I love to eat, but I usually eat my big meal at noontime."

"When we fly to Grand Cayman, I'll remember that. We usually have a lot to eat on the boat for the divers, so I don't think you'll starve." He cut into his salmon and chewed it slowly, as if he were savoring it.

"I've always wanted to see Grand Cayman. What's it like?" Marnie asked when she had finished half her main course, all her senses reacting to the man across from her.

"It's beautiful. I own a villa there that I use part of the year. It's a peaceful place to write. Never the bother of a big city. But then I always come back to New York."

"I must confess that until today I hadn't read your books. I picked up three of them at the library and read one this afternoon. You're good." Marnie fingered the rim of her water glass.

Laughing, he said, "If hiring you converted you to a

16

Damon Wilson reader, then I'm glad I offered you the job."

"This will be your sixth book. Each subject has been so different from the others. What made you pick treasure hunting?"

"I love to dive and I'd been researching a previous book when I ran across some evidence that indicates there might be a sunken Spanish galleon near the coast of Little Cayman. So I traced this ship's path through some old data and have determined approximately where it went down in a hurricane hundreds of years ago. The *Santa Santiago* was separated from a sister ship near the Cayman Islands during the storm and was never heard of since. There were a few survivors from the *Santa Santiago* who made it to shore on Little Cayman and their accounts of their ordeal were recorded in the Spanish Colonial Archives in Seville. That's how I got started on this project, but I'm not always sure how each of my ideas comes to me. However, they have brought me an interest in life and some small material success of my own."

Small success, Marnie thought. *I'd say more like millions.*

As she sipped her coffee, she scanned the dining room once more. Suddenly Marnie stiffened in her chair, a sudden coldness numbing her senses. She turned away from the couple who had entered the dining room, but not before she noticed that Anita had seen her.

Maybe they won't come by the table, Marnie told herself.

But when Robert and Anita approached them a few minutes later, Marnie clenched her hands in her lap. She breathed deeply, then looked up at her stepsister.

"I didn't expect to see you here, Marnie," her

stepsister said, purring. Anita turned her attention to Damon. A slow smile moved across her features as she extended her hand to him. "I'm Anita Bradley, Marnie's sister."

Damon stood and took her hand, holding it longer than necessary. Marnie's stomach knotted with tension.

"Good to see you again, Robert," Marnie said as she noticed her stepsister's intense concentration on Damon.

"How have you been, Marnie?" Robert whispered. "I've been meaning to call you and explain, but . . ."

"There's nothing to explain, Robert," Marnie responded quietly, then added, "You preferred Anita to me, that's all. Have a lovely evening." She dismissed him with a cold smile.

When Anita and Robert walked away, Marnie sensed Damon's gaze boring into her. Turning, she looked deeply into those gray eyes, almost silver with the lights of the room shining in their depths.

"Your sister is charming," he said, the expression in his eyes masked by his thick black lashes. "Why is she called Anita Bradley? Is she married to that man she was with?"

"She's my stepsister," Marnie muttered. A feeling of dejection claimed her. "And no, she isn't married to Robert."

At the end of the meal Damon pushed back his chair and stood. "I've enjoyed the evening, but it's been a very long day, Marnie." He helped her from her chair and guided her toward the front door, his whisper-soft touch warm, intimate.

"But we haven't even talked about the assignment! That was the purpose of this dinner, Mr. Wilson."

"Damon, please. Yes, it was, but we can go over the

18

details on the flight to Grand Cayman. Can you be ready to leave in one week?"

"Yes."

"Good. Then I'll pick you up at your apartment next Tuesday morning at eight and we'll fly down to the island. I'll take care of all the arrangements. You just be ready with your equipment."

They waited as the chauffeur double-parked the limousine in front of the restaurant. On the ride to her apartment Marnie wanted to ask a hundred questions about the island and the assignment, her interest aroused. Slanting a glance at Damon, she saw the furrowed brows, the thinned lips tightly drawn together as if he were lost in deep thought, and she knew the questions would have to wait until another time.

As the limousine drew to a halt outside her apartment building, Damon reached across her lap and opened the door for her before the chauffeur could get out of the car. They briefly touched, and Marnie felt seared by the brush of his arm.

As she stepped out onto the curb, she heard Damon say, "Good night, Marnie. Be ready next Tuesday."

Then the limousine sped away, disappearing from her view. She stared down the street for a long moment before she walked into the building.

After Marnie pressed the button on the elevator for the third floor, she hugged her arms to herself. *I hope I don't regret going to Grand Cayman.*

Chapter Two

"Carolyn, I can't believe I have so much to do in three days' time. I must refresh my memory on the techniques of scuba diving. If Damon Wilson found out the last time I dived, he would have my head." Marnie walked into her kitchen and looked back through the living room door. "Would you like something to drink?"

After settling herself on a bar stool, Carolyn stated, "Something warm. The weather is getting beastly outside. I hate to think it's only November and we still have four more months of cold weather. I sure do envy you going to the Caribbean in a few days. Think of all that hot weather and beautiful, warm sunshine."

"I doubt he'll let me do much relaxing in the sun." Marnie laughed. "I have a feeling he's a hard man to work for." Marnie placed a kettle of water on the stove, then turned back to Carolyn. "*Is* he hard to work for, Carolyn? You know more about him than I do. What are those stories you heard about Damon?"

"I don't think I should tell you. It's only gossip anyway, Marnie." An anxious note entered Carolyn's voice as a frown creased her forehead.

Marnie dropped a tea bag into each cup, then faced Carolyn. "From the tone of your voice I would say what you've heard isn't flattering. Am I correct?" She raised a brow. "Carolyn, you've never kept anything from me before—why now?"

Carolyn studied the beige tiles covering the top of the bar.

"Carolyn."

"Okay," Carolyn whispered, and looked up at Marnie. "Okay, I'll tell you what I've heard. It really isn't much." Carolyn paused and inhaled deeply before continuing. "He's a womanizer. He never stays long with any one woman. And when he leaves them, he can be quite heartless. Marnie, I know you've been hurt recently, so be careful."

"Thanks for the warning. I can't see me falling for anyone now—especially someone like Damon Wilson. I've been *burned* and don't care to live through that experience again."

"But that's just one side to him, Marnie. He's a very complex man. Just a few weeks ago I found out he donates all the money he receives from his book *A Deadly Trap* to an orphanage here in New York City." Carolyn bent forward. "When he's in town, he spends every Friday at the orphanage. It's hard to believe a busy man like him can find the time."

The kettle whistled, a high shrill sound that pierced the air. Marnie turned and busied herself pouring water into the cups. She imagined the man she had had dinner with playing with the children at the orphanage, laughing, teasing with them. *Yes,* Marnie thought. *He likes children. You can tell that from his books.*

When she passed a cup through the opening to Carolyn, the older woman asked, "Has Damon Wilson called you since you went out to dinner with him that night?"

Marnie stirred a spoonful of sugar into her tea and watched the steam waft to the ceiling for a moment before answering, "No. All I know is that I must be ready by Tuesday. I really don't know much else about this assignment. We'll be on a boat off the coast of Little Cayman and we'll be searching for a sunken Spanish galleon." Marnie shrugged. "The rest you can guess along with me."

"He's good though, Marnie. If your name is connected with his book, you'll be able to write your own ticket. Remember that that's what you're looking for."

Marnie leaned against the cabinet. "I know. I just hope it's enough. Somehow I get this feeling when I start to think about him." Her voice lowered. "Thinking about him causes queasiness in the pit of my stomach."

With a quick glance at her watch, Carolyn bolted to her feet and exclaimed, "Oh, Marnie, I'm late again. Won't I ever learn to be on time for appointments? I'll see you when you get back in a month. Have a good time. Take some great pictures." She smiled and waved before going out the door.

Turning the lock on her door, Marnie listened as it clicked into place, then spun around and scanned the disarray of her living room. Photographic equipment was scattered all over the floor. With a deep sigh she leaned against the door and relished a quiet moment before she straightened and moved into the center of the mess.

She collapsed into a chair and stretched her legs out

in front of her, then rested her head on the back cushion and stared at the ceiling. *You could back out of this assignment without too much trouble, Marnie,* she told herself. *It would be safer for you.* Sitting up straight, she slowly moved her head from side to side. *No, that would get Carolyn in trouble with Mr. Morrison, and besides, I don't think I could face Damon Wilson and tell him I wasn't going—not at the last minute this way. I do need the job.*

When a loud knock sounded at the door, Marnie sat upright. She tilted her head to one side and whispered, "Now who could that be?"

Crossing the living room to the door, Marnie checked through the peephole and stiffened when she saw Anita standing in the hallway.

Marnie opened the door, a frown etched into her features. "I thought you got everything you needed the last time, Anita. What else do you want—I've already given you my boyfriend, half my clothes . . ."

As Anita walked into the apartment, she smiled. "I just came by to see how you were getting along." She whirled and faced Marnie, her stepsister's golden eyes glittering with curiosity. "Where are you going?"

Marnie closed the front door and stepped into the living room. The muscles in her stomach tightened as she braced herself against Anita's too-sweet voice.

"Going? What makes you think I'm going anywhere?" Her brows lifted in mock surprise.

"You're getting all your equipment ready for some trip. I can tell."

Marnie forced herself to laugh. "What concern is that of yours?"

"I want those photographs done of me for my modeling portfolio. You promised and you know you don't go back on your word."

23

"Unlike some people I know." Sitting down, Marnie glanced through a pile of photographs.

Anita ignored the remark and sat down. She smoothed her silver-blond hair into place and scanned the room once more. "Must be an important job. You're taking every piece of equipment you own."

"Anita, I don't have time for small talk. I'll take those photographs of you when I finish this assignment."

"When will that be, Marnie?"

"In a few months."

"A few months! But I need them now."

"I'm sorry, but that's as soon as I can do it."

Anita pouted, her features childlike. "You know Robert has gotten me several jobs with his magazine. That should help me. I might not need your photographs by the time you get back."

Anita rose and examined herself in the mirror over the mantel. She tossed her shoulder-length hair behind her and smiled a fake smile that didn't reach her topaz eyes. "Robert is quite good at a lot of things, but then you wouldn't know about that. You were always the good little girl. The apple of my daddy's eye. You could never do anything wrong." Anita continued to talk to her image in the mirror as she arranged her features into different poses. "You'll never hold a man's interest for long. Men get bored with innocence."

Marnie wanted to cross the room and shake some sense into her stepsister, but instead she consciously arranged her features into an impassive expression.

"I got the hand-me-downs. You got the brand-new things. You got to go to college, while I had to work," Anita said in her syrupy voice.

"Anita, you know I would have helped you through college. You didn't want to go. Instead you had to come to New York and live with me. You wanted to launch your modeling career. Remember?"

Anita pursed her lips as if she were going to kiss her reflection in the mirror, then she relaxed the pose and turned to face Marnie. "It doesn't matter now. I'm on my way and I did it all by myself without your help. I'll be rich and famous one day, while you'll be struggling to make a name for yourself in a man's world. Good luck, big 'sis.'" Anita gathered up her purse and started for the door, halting halfway across the living room when the doorbell sounded.

"Expecting someone, Marnie? A man perhaps?" Anita tossed her purse onto the sofa. "I think I'll stay and see for myself."

"I don't think that's necessary," Marnie said over her shoulder as she reached the door. Then leaning close to the door she called out, "Yes? Can I help you?"

"You might start by opening the door," came the deep, rich reply.

Color drained from Marnie's cheeks. She hesitated before placing her hand on the doorknob.

"Well, Marnie, aren't you going to do what the man says? Open the door. I want to see this new man of yours." Her stepsister moved nearer the front door, a look of anticipation flashing across her features.

Marnie twisted the knob and pulled the door toward her. She forced herself to smile and say lightly, "What can I do for you, Mr. Wilson?"

"Damon, remember? First I would like to be invited in." His voice was a slow, lazy drawl. After a quick sweeping appraisal of Marnie, Damon turned his attention to Anita. His look, encompassing every feature of Anita's face, suddenly became very male, very suggestive. Without waiting for an invitation, he stepped into the apartment.

"So we meet again." Damon took Anita's hand and kissed the back of it before he slowly released his grasp, his raking gaze missing nothing.

After closing the door, Marnie cleared her throat and walked into the living room, suddenly feeling like an intruder in her own apartment. In faded blue jeans and a light blue turtleneck sweater she definitely felt unsophisticated next to her stepsister.

"I'd hoped I would meet you again. I never told you how much I enjoyed *A Deadly Trap*," Anita said.

Standing by the mantel, Marnie stiffened as her stepsister smiled at Damon, Anita's lips curling in that seductive way that she had when she was after a man.

Marnie stepped forward. "Didn't you say you had something to attend to, Anita?"

Anita raised an eyebrow and with a laugh said, "No. Whatever made you think that?" Anita guided Damon to the sofa and sat next to him.

Marnie glared at her stepsister, her anger building until she thought she would explode.

"May I help you, Mr. Wilson?" Marnie finally managed to ask when she got her temper under control, a fragile control that threatened to snap at the least provocation.

Damon dragged his gaze from Anita to look at Marnie, an armor of indifference falling over his dark features.

"Help me?" His brows wrinkled in thought. "Oh, yes. I was through earlier than expected, so I thought I would take you to dinner—that is, if you haven't already eaten."

"I have." Marnie sounded angrier than she had wanted to, but she was bothered by seeing Anita's hand resting on Damon's arm.

"I thought we might discuss the assignment, but I haven't eaten all day . . ."

"Then let me show you a restaurant I know not too far from here that has the best Italian food," Anita cut in.

Damon swung his attention to Anita, his mouth set in a smile. "That sounds good. My chauffeur is downstairs waiting in front of the building. I'd like to have a word with Marnie alone first. Go and wait in the limousine."

Anita's mouth formed a pout, but she hesitantly rose, walked to the door, and opened it, glancing back at Damon and flashing him a brilliant smile. "Don't be too long," she said, purring.

When the door closed, all Marnie could hear was the ticking of the clock over the mantel. She turned from Damon and busied herself with her camera.

"What do you want?" She tried to sound bored, uninterested, but her voice was breathless.

"Since I was able to finish my business earlier than planned, I thought we would fly to Grand Cayman tomorrow afternoon. That still gives you the morning to finish packing."

Marnie knew he wasn't asking her. His words were stated as an order. Suddenly she exploded. "I've decided not to take the assignment. Find someone else, Mr. Wilson."

His gray eyes turned the color of a sea storm. The muscles in his neck tensed, his jaw became rigid.

In a quiet voice he repeated, "Find someone else." He waved his arm. "Just like that. Well, for your information, Miss Stevens, you signed a contract, and I'll hold you to it."

"I don't want to do this assignment. It's not for me. I haven't dived in seven years." She lifted her chin in determination.

His eyes became pinpoints as he folded his arms across his chest and lounged against the chair. Marnie

27

felt her arguments evaporate as he stared at her, his expression too neutral. The air vibrated with the silence that hung between them. She remembered the deadly calm of the eye of a hurricane and steeled herself for the storm.

Finally, he said, "I know you haven't been diving since you lived in New Smyrna Beach. I also know that you became interested in photography while diving. Believe me, if I didn't think you were right for my book, you wouldn't have the job." Dropping his arms to his sides, he advanced toward Marnie. A heavily veiled look stole over his dark features. "I know all about you. I make it a habit to find out about employees who will be staying with me while working on a project."

Shocked, Marnie's eyes widened. "Staying with you?"

"Yes, at my villa when we aren't on the boat working, diving."

Marnie's shock receded into apprehension. "No."

He drew closer, his face just inches from hers. "What do you mean, no?" Again his voice was quiet. A coldness within it chilled Marnie to the bone.

"I'd rather stay at a hotel." He unnerved her with the way he looked at her. It made her feel as if he were making love to her with his eyes.

He tossed back his head and roared with laughter. "Do you think I would ravish you? Hardly. You needn't worry about that, Miss Stevens. You aren't my type."

She tried to make herself seem taller than her five feet three inches, but he continued to tower over her, making her feel vulnerable.

"It's the height of the tourist season and all rooms have been booked for months. Miss Stevens, you won't be alone with me, so you needn't worry."

Desperately she asked, "How can you still have me as your photographer if you know I haven't been diving in years?"

"Because you're good and I want to get started on this project immediately. I don't have time to search for someone else. I believe with a little practice your memory will be refreshed." His breath tangled with hers. "I'm an excellent teacher." The warmth of his breath tickled her cheek, his heady male scent an erotic drug.

"Damon." Anita stood in the doorway.

Marnie looked over Damon's shoulder at her stepsister, Anita's hands on her waist and a pout on her face. Damon glanced at Anita, his eyes glinting with a metallic sheen.

"Damon, I'm starved. Aren't you coming?" Anita's body curved in a provocative pose.

"Yes. Yes. Wait at the elevator," Damon said, his voice laced with impatience.

When Anita had disappeared, Marnie glared at Damon. "Take her, I'm not going. Find someone else!" She put the distance of a few feet between them and inhaled a gulp of air. "Anita's your type. Teach her to take pictures."

"Must I remind you that you've signed a contract, Miss Stevens?"

Marnie stared into his steel-gray eyes. His eyes were like shards of ice. Not trusting herself to speak, she shook her head in reply.

He stepped closer until his lips touched hers. "I'm glad we understand each other—Marnie." He whispered her name against her mouth, a soft caress that wrapped Marnie in a blanket of warmth.

He nibbled an earlobe, then brushed his lips across the hollow at the base of her throat. When he possessed her mouth in a long, deep kiss, Marnie felt the air forced from her lungs as if she were drowning and fighting for her last breath. She struggled to retain control of her senses.

Marnie tried to wriggle free of his ironclad hold, but he just tightened his grip on her wrists as he continued to overwhelm her with his soft, sensual kisses. Her flesh tingled where he kissed her. A moan escaped her lips, and she knew she was helpless to stop him. *And I'm not sure I want to,* flashed through her mind.

When Damon pulled away, Marnie gasped for a breath. Confusion tumbled through her mind as she stared at him crossing the room and opening the front door. Conflicting emotions flickered across her features. Disappointment? Relief?

"Be ready tomorrow afternoon. My chauffeur will pick you up at two o'clock," Damon said in a deep, raspy voice.

No words would form in Marnie's mind as he closed the door and she collapsed into a nearby chair. She felt so alone. Her legs were like water, her heart madly pumping the blood through her body. Brushing her fingers across her kiss-swollen lips, she imagined his tongue probing the depths of her mouth again. Shivering, she hugged her body as chills covered her flesh.

Heartless. Cruel. Arrogant. Words leaped into her thoughts. She knew she would have to be very careful in the next few months if she were going to emerge from this assignment in one piece.

Taking in a deep breath, Marnie, as she stood, looked at the pile of photographic equipment and slowly shook her head. *I'll just finish my packing tomorrow morning. I can't face doing it now,* she said to herself as she walked into her bedroom and undressed.

When she had crawled between the warm covers of her bed, she found herself staring at the ceiling, her eyes wide open. Visions of Damon Wilson and Anita danced in the darkness before her. She rubbed her eyes, but still she could imagine them laughing and dancing together, holding each other in a tight clasp.

She became a hard core of nerves as she tried to banish the images from her mind. "Why do you always want what you think is mine?" Marnie asked the imaginary figure of her stepsister.

As Marnie waited for a response that would never come, the clock chimed two times. She rolled onto her side and pulled the covers over her head. Sleep finally descended, a restless sleep that left Marnie battered and tired the next morning.

As Marnie searched for her slippers, the loud ringing of the phone startled her. She reached for the receiver and in her haste knocked it off its cradle. Retrieving the phone from the floor, she answered it.

"Good morning, big 'sis.' Did you sleep well? I slept wonderfully. I'm just calling to thank you for introducing me to Damon. He's divine," Anita said with a soft laugh that made Marnie clench the receiver tightly.

Gathering the shreds of her composure, Marnie said in a calm voice, "I don't have time to talk, Anita. I must be packed and ready to go in just a few hours. Good-bye." She replaced the phone in its cradle and stared at it, the words Anita had said taunting her.

Why should I care? Why am I so upset? she asked herself.

When the phone rang again a few minutes later, Marnie grabbed the receiver and said breathlessly, "Yes," half expecting Anita to be on the other end.

"Marnie?" The rich timbre of his voice sent a wave of chills through her.

"Yes, Damon. What do you want? I think we have said enough to each other for the time being. I'll be ready at two this afternoon, but only if you let me start packing *now*." She winced at her own harsh-sounding voice, her feelings confusing her.

"Did I wake you or something?"

"No."

"Are you always this nasty early in the morning? If so, the crew and I are in for some stormy days at sea." He paused, a lengthy silence stretching between them.

In a calmer voice Marnie asked, "What can I do for you?"

"I was just calling to tell you that my chauffeur will be an hour late. It's an hour that I know you can use. He'll be there at three. Good day."

Marnie sat holding the phone as the dial tone greeted her ear. Paling, she slowly placed the receiver in its cradle as his brisk, impersonal words assailed her. She felt about an inch tall and wanted to crawl back under the covers and hide the rest of the day.

He's just my employer. He means nothing else to me. Anita can have him, she said to herself.

Marnie rose from the bed and walked toward the bathroom. *I'll show him what a good photographer I am. That's all I need to do,* she told herself. But she recalled the pure masculine sensuality that surrounded Damon Wilson and knew it wouldn't be an easy job.

"Just remember Robert," she whispered.

The skyline of Manhattan disappeared from Marnie's view before she reclined back in her seat and released her pent-up breath. Surveying the cabin of Damon's Lear jet, she noted its plush velour-covered seats and several tables for playing cards or working.

The jet continued to rise until only white fluffy clouds surrounded it. With eyes closed, Marnie let the soothing lull of the ride relax her raw nerves.

She relived the morning packing in her mind, going through her automatic actions again. By the time the chauffeur had appeared at her front door, she had been exhausted, unable to move, but then she remembered how much she needed the job and forced herself to place one foot in front of the other.

"Do you have all the equipment you'll need to take those underwater shots I want?" Damon's voice disturbed her musing and Marnie looked up into his face, his features set in a neutral expression. Tilting her head to one side to give him a look of inquiry, she said, "Yes?"

"Do you have all the equipment you need? Since you haven't dived in years, I thought you might not have what you require," he repeated.

"Yes. I have everything I will need."

Damon sat in the seat next to hers. "Good. When we get to the villa, I want to go over the procedures for diving with you. We'll start searching for the wreck in two days. I don't want any problems when we get out on the boat, so we'll use my swimming pool to refresh your memory on diving."

"A swimming pool when you have the ocean?" Marnie stared wide-eyed at Damon.

A frown touched his features. "The swimming pool will be safer. Or have you forgotten the dangers of diving? You may be certified, but that was *years* ago."

Marnie's throat closed as anger consumed her. "I do know how dangerous diving can be, Mr. Wilson." She twisted in her seat and looked out the window, watching the blue and white blur of the sky speed by.

"Miss Stevens," he continued, his voice even, with only a hint of coldness in it. "I'll want pictures of everything having to do with this salvage from the beginning to the end. This project may prove to take a

33

year if what I believe is on the *Santa Santiago* exists. I'll want you to record the history of the galleon through each of the artifacts we find."

"A year? I was led to believe only a few months for this assignment. I can't . . ."

"You won't spend the whole year in the water or on the boat—only one week a month after the salvage is under way. I'll fly you back and forth from New York." He examined her face before he continued. "I want you to develop your pictures at night and have them ready for my inspection the next day. I'll select what I need from what you've shot. I'll also make suggestions on shots you need to take."

"Suggestions?" She stared out the window.

Grasping her arm, Damon placed his other hand under her chin and pulled her head around. Marnie was compelled to look him in the eye.

"If the word *order* suits you better, then I'll order what shots I want you to take." He swept his gaze over Marnie before standing. "You can make this assignment enjoyable or miserable. Since we're going to spend some time together in close quarters with each other, I *suggest* both of us remain civil."

Before Marnie could retort, Damon turned and walked toward the pilot's cabin. She glared at him until she could no longer see him.

"That arrogant man!" Marnie whispered, her heart pounding against her breasts. "I'll be civil and polite, but *that is all.*"

Marnie's intense emotions drained what little strength she had left. She leaned next to the wall with a small pillow and closed her eyes to sleep. The hypnotic humming of the jet engine drew her rapidly toward the blackness.

"Wake up, Marnie!" A voice reached down into the darkness and pulled her toward the daylight.

Someone was shaking her shoulder.

"Marnie, we're arriving at the airport on Grand Cayman. Get up." Damon's voice coaxed her from her sleep.

Marnie sat up and stifled a yawn with her hand. When she turned to look at Damon, her breath caught in her throat at his handsome features with only a trace of his earlier coldness in his eyes.

Marnie looked out the window and saw the muted colors of dusk as the jet neared the runway. As Damon sat in the seat beside her, his raw maleness brought a shiver rippling through her. Disturbed by his nearness, Marnie snapped her seat belt together and braced herself for the landing.

Damon took one look at her stiff arms and hands that gripped the seat and smiled, all harshness fleeing as laugh lines appeared at the corners of his eyes. "Don't tell me you're scared of flying? A girl who loved to race cars on the weekend when she was in college?"

"How did you know about that?"

"I make it a habit to find out things, Marnie. Remember?"

"All you have to know is that I'm good at taking photographs. The rest is none of your business." The minute Marnie spoke she regretted her words. The smile on Damon's face vanished to be replaced by a frown. He turned straight ahead and remained silent throughout the landing.

Marnie forgot her apprehension about the jet's landing as she looked sidelong at Damon's grim features. *Why did you say that?* she asked herself. *You already knew he had checked you out. He does have a right to know about his employees.* Marnie found herself wondering what was in that report about her. *He knows about my love for racing. What else does he know?*

The wheels making contact with the landing strip

brought Marnie out of her musing. She buried her fingernails into the palms of her hands until the jet was safely on the ground.

As she relaxed, she looked out the window into the darkness. There were a few lights, but nothing else. She shrugged off her disappointment. *I'll have enough time to see the island later,* she thought, and rose. She leaned on the seat in front of her for support until her legs stopped quivering.

As Damon started to move away, she caught his arm and pulled him around to look at her. Staring into those gray eyes of his, she said, "I was out of line with what I said. Sorry."

He didn't say anything in response to her apology, his features neutral as he studied her. His unwavering gaze seemed to be probing her innermost thoughts as he drew her closer and bent his head toward her. Suddenly she wanted him to kiss her. She yearned for his mouth to caress hers again in that soft, sensual way of his. But when he was only inches from her face, he pulled back and turned away.

"We have a lot to do. Let's get going," he said.

Her cheeks flamed, her mouth opened slightly, frustration overwhelming her as she followed Damon from the jet.

Chapter Three

Inhaling a deep breath of air saturated with the salty tang of the sea, Marnie listened to the water breaking against the rocky shoreline only yards away from Damon's villa. She stared toward the darkness of the ocean. A night bird trilled softly in the distance.

Moving toward the sound of the sea, she stood on the edge of a cliff overlooking the water. Damon touched her shoulder, but she continued to look out across the moonlit water. She felt the magnetic pull of the ocean, the cool breeze ruffling her hair. Blond strands whipped across her face.

"I often like to come out here near sundown and watch the sun sink below the horizon. It's something you shouldn't miss. It's one of the breathtaking beauties of nature that words can never fully describe," Damon said, his voice unusually husky.

As she leaned into his muscled firmness, she relished

the strong pressure of his hand on her shoulder. Marnie heard the water striking the rocky beach below them and memories of her childhood in Florida crept into her mind. Happy memories, fun-filled memories. She felt as if she had come home at last. A warmth coursed through her veins.

Turning, Marnie caught sight of Damon's handsome features illuminated in silvery radiance. She was overwhelmed by the man's powerful force. Stepping away, she almost lost her footing, rocks crumbling under her left foot as she clutched for the nearest steady thing, Damon. His strong hands gripped her about the waist and swung her away from the cliff. When she was safe, he dropped his arms to his sides. She shuddered and pressed closer to him as she thought of the fall to the rocks below. At first he held his arms stiff at his sides, then slowly his arms encircled Marnie, his touch reassuring, his steady heartbeat soothing.

Marnie tilted her head back to gaze into his face. Their eyes met and his metallic gaze captured her dark one. Parting her mouth slightly, she welcomed his lips upon hers. He cradled her face within his hands and brushed his lips across hers, leaving a trail of whisper-soft kisses as he moved his mouth to tease her earlobe.

Marnie sucked in her ragged breath and tried to calm the racing of her heartbeat, but with each caress of his mouth upon her flesh she felt her self-control slip away from her.

She closed her eyes as his mouth roamed over her face, neck, and shoulders. Her mouth tingled where she could imagine the velvet warmth of his lips possessing hers. And when he finally kissed her on the mouth, she wanted it as she had never wanted anything before. Marnie felt dizzy as his lips bruised hers in a demanding kiss that drew the strength from her. Then his lips were no longer touching hers. She opened her eyes and watched him as he turned away from her.

"Tomorrow is a big day. You'd better get your rest. We'll begin working out in the pool at eight sharp." He started to walk toward the house with lithe gracefulness.

Perplexed, Marnie stood rooted to the ground, realizing she would have surrendered to him if he hadn't pulled away. *That mustn't happen again*, she thought, but memories of his kisses made that vow sound hollow.

Turning back, he called, "Aren't you coming?"

She hurried after him, her heartbeat no longer under control as her heart madly pounded against her ribs. As she approached the two-story villa, most of the house was shrouded in darkness. A light near the entrance beckoned Marnie toward it.

When they stepped into the hallway, Marnie felt as if she had entered another world. The first thing she saw when her eyes adjusted to the brightness of the light was the winding staircase that led to the second floor. Deep yellow wallpaper with white ferns covered the entrance hall walls. A gleaming chandelier with crystal and polished brass fixtures hung from the two-story ceiling of the foyer.

Damon pulled Marnie toward a doorway, but she seemed to be in a trance as she entered the living room and saw the moonlight glittering off the sea a hundred yards from the villa through the floor-to-ceiling windows along one wall. In a slow turn she noted the richness of her surroundings in the white velvet sofas, the kelly green chairs, the white plush carpet, paintings hanging on the walls, and the glass figurines that accented the room.

"I knew your books had been best sellers, but this is

beyond what I had dreamed." Marnie threw out her arms to gesture at the beauty around her.

Damon walked to the bar and took a glass from the cabinet. "Would you care for a drink?"

She shook her head.

"Writing began as a hobby for me. Now it's a passion. Before I started writing, though, I ran Eastern Communications, Marnie."

"Eastern Communications! Why, they own newspapers, television stations, radio stations. You name it in the communication field and they have a part in it. What made you start writing? Do you have anything to do with the company now?"

"Yes, I still have the final say, since I own the controlling stock, but it isn't my whole life like it once was. My father built the company into the conglomerate that it is today from a chain of newspapers that my grandfather had started. I got bored with high finance and the business world, so I turned to writing. Now it's a part of my life that I can't do without."

Marnie walked to the bar and sat on a stool. "I know what you mean. That's the way I feel about my photography. I love to capture a moment in time on film and preserve it forever. Much the same way you do with words."

With her chin cupped in her hand, Marnie rested her elbow on the bar. "But if you own the Eastman Publishing House, why do you have an agent? You don't need him. You have it made with your very own publishing firm."

A frown narrowed Damon's eyes. "Marnie, I used Bert Morrison as my agent because I didn't want my name to influence the publishing of my first book. I wanted to make it on my own without the Wilson name. It wouldn't have meant much the other way.

Bert represented me without knowing who I was at first. Now he manages that end of my affairs for me. He's well worth the money I pay him."

Marnie felt the sting of his words, her cheeks becoming hot with embarrassment. She muttered, "I think I'll take that drink after all. Water, please."

When Damon handed Marnie her glass of ice water, their hands touched for a second. Her reaction to the warmth of his fingers brushing hers deepened the color in her cheeks. She gulped down the icy liquid in four swallows.

"I'm tired. Which room is mine?" Marnie stared at the empty glass.

"I had Mrs. Carson prepare the guest bedroom. It's the first door on the right when you go up the stairs." He flicked his hand in the direction of the staircase and dismissed her with the tone of his voice.

"Where are my suitcases?"

"They're in your room by now. James has no doubt unloaded the car."

"James?" Marnie asked, unable to believe that someone had entered the house after them, carrying their luggage.

"James and Mrs. Carson look after the house for me. I told you in New York you wouldn't be alone. They both live in apartments at the back of the house."

"Oh," was all Marnie could manage to say before she stood and made her way toward the staircase.

She found her bedroom with no problem. Closing the door, she saw the suitcases in the middle of the spacious room surrounded by white furniture and a cool green carpet as plush as the one downstairs in the living room. After she tossed her purse on the floral green bedspread, Marnie walked to the door nearest her.

When Marnie opened the door, she gasped at the

large bathroom with a sunken bathtub dominating the room in the center. Again green and white colored the towels, the walls, and the tiles.

Weariness claimed her. Moving to the sink, Marnie turned on the tap. She splashed some water onto her face and felt its cool freshness. With a sigh, she walked back into the bedroom and opened the other door in the room. As she stepped into the room-size closet, she laughed.

"There's no way I could begin to fill that closet," she said aloud as she reentered the bedroom.

She sank into a green velvet chair and kicked off her shoes. Wiggling her toes in the softness of the carpet, she leaned back to rest her head on the cushion. *What am I doing here?* she wondered. *This is just another job for me,* she repeated to herself, but somehow she couldn't quite convince herself that all she cared about was the job.

When Marnie awoke, sunlight streamed through the sliding glass door. Refreshed from a good night's sleep, she climbed out of bed and walked to the sliding glass door and stepped outside into the salty air. A warm breeze whipped the hem of her nightgown about her ankles. She threw back her head and let the rays of the sun strike her face.

Contentment flowed through her veins for a long moment until she heard a deep voice say, "Good morning, Marnie. I don't think you're quite dressed for a diving lesson."

Marnie turned in the direction that the voice came from and smiled at the amusement that lit Damon's features. Then she saw his gaze travel the length of her and realized too late that she was clad only in a thin, nylon nightgown that left little to the imagination.

Marnie stood frozen for a moment staring into

Damon's laughing eyes. Then she brought a hand up to suppress a startled cry before she turned around and quickly walked back inside.

She yanked the draperies across the glass door and sank into a chair. As she listened to his laughter, she covered herself with folded arms. She felt hot and cold at the same time as she remembered his gray eyes sparkling with unconcealed desire.

Carolyn's words came back to haunt Marnie. "He's a womanizer. Be careful, Marnie."

That I plan to be, she thought as she rose and dressed in an aquamarine one-piece swimming suit with a low neckline and a cutout back. After slipping a white terry cloth cover-up over her bathing suit, she slid her feet into thongs, then made her way down the stairs to the living room.

As she turned around to decide which direction the kitchen was in, Damon appeared in the doorway. He was dressed in a white sports shirt and red shorts, his sinewy muscular legs braced apart, his arms folded across his chest.

"Good morning again." His smile widened. "You don't seem to be very friendly in the morning. Maybe I should have you awakened an hour before everyone else, so by the time we see you you're in a good mood."

"Very funny. You know very well . . ." Marnie paused and watched Damon trying to contain his laughter but doing a poor job of it as he doubled over with laughter.

She turned and walked toward the nearest door. Again she felt her embarrassment color her cheeks. *He's not going to do this to me again,* she said to herself. *I won't have him making a fool of me every time I turn around. I blush like a schoolgirl in love for the first time whenever he says anything to me.*

Marnie glanced around the dining room, then pushed open a swinging door. She entered the kitchen and scanned the sparkling clean area, everything in its proper place. A plump woman turned from the counter and faced Marnie. A smile spread across the older woman's face, causing the hint of a dimple to appear in her cheek.

"I'm Marnie Stevens." Marnie held out her hand to the woman with gray hair pulled back into a tight bun at the nape of her neck.

The woman's face crinkled into a wider grin. "I'm Mrs. Carson, the housekeeper, cook. You name it, I do it around here."

"Damon said I would be meeting you this morning. I just came in here for a cup of coffee before I head for the swimming pool."

Mrs. Carson gestured toward a tray sitting on the countertop. "I was going to bring you a light breakfast in your room. Most of Mr. Wilson's—er—guests prefer breakfast in their rooms."

I wonder how many are women guests, Marnie thought, then aloud said, "I'll just come to the kitchen every morning."

Mrs. Carson's brown eyes widened, but she quickly masked her startled expression by busying herself with picking up the tray.

"Well, if you'll have a seat, I'll be glad to cook you something."

Marnie sat at the kitchen table and sipped the steaming coffee. "Just a piece of toast for right now. I don't want to swim on a full stomach."

"Very wise, Marnie."

Marnie swung her head around and saw Damon lounging against the doorjamb. Advancing into the kitchen, the corners of his mouth turned up in a smile packed with his male charm.

44

"Good morning, Mrs. Carson. I'll take a cup of coffee and a sweet roll," Damon said.

"I have a letter from Amy for you, Mr. Wilson. And she wanted me to give you this picture she drew." Mrs. Carson withdrew a folded piece of paper from her apron pocket and handed it to Damon before moving to the coffeepot to pour a cup for him. "The doctors say she'll have to stay in the hospital." The woman's eyes filled with tears. "Thank you again for your help. My sister didn't know where she would get the money until you gave her a job. She . . ."

Embarrassed, Damon waved his hand and interrupted, "Thank you for this picture. I'll go see Amy."

"She'll like that," Mrs. Carson mumbled, and wiped the tears away with the hem of her apron.

Damon sat in the chair next to Marnie and looked at her. "Did you sleep all right last night?" he asked as Mrs. Carson handed him a cup of coffee and a sweet roll.

Marnie stared at Damon for a moment, her mind still dwelling on the conversation between him and Mrs. Carson. She saw Damon's nervous fidgeting and knew he hadn't wanted her to witness their exchange.

"Marnie?" Damon tapped her hand with a spoon.

"I'd forgotten how wonderful the sound of the surf can be when you're falling asleep. It's like music, soft and hypnotic," she answered.

"I find I like this house best of all. Living near the ocean can be the best medicine in the world, Marnie, when you're having trouble sleeping."

As Marnie hurriedly ate her piece of toast, she listened to Mrs. Carson humming while she was cleaning up the kitchen. Marnie avoided looking at Damon but instead watched a seabird fly past the kitchen window.

Who's Amy? Marnie wondered. *What's wrong with her?* Marnie chewed the last bite of her toast slowly, then washed it down with some coffee.

After breakfast Marnie and Damon walked to the cabana next to the pool and Marnie waited outside while Damon went inside to get the diving equipment. Marnie looked out across the turquoise-blue sea and saw several motorboats speeding away from the island.

When she heard a noise behind her, she turned to face Damon. He handed her a pair of fins, a face mask, and a weight belt. She looked at the equipment. *I hope I remember everything,* she thought. She consciously composed her features into an expression of confidence.

Marnie slipped her feet into the flippers, then placed the mask on her face. She buckled the weight belt around her waist and allowed Damon to help her with her buoyancy-compensator vest and her breathing tank.

Damon turned on the valve and said, "Gas on."

Marnie bit the mouthpiece and blew out once before she took several deep breaths on the regulator. She entered the water and waded to chest level, then sat on the bottom of the pool. Taking deep breaths, she turned on her stomach and began to swim. When she felt her body being pulled toward the bottom, she surfaced and climbed out of the water.

"What's wrong?" Damon asked, his brows furrowed.

"Too much weight." Marnie adjusted the weight on her belt, then reentered the water.

This time she found herself swimming through the water like a bird soaring through the sky. She relished the feel of isolation and quiet. While she arched her back slightly to keep from touching the bottom, she lapped the pool several times.

When she surfaced, Damon called out to her, "Take

off your mask underwater, then replace it and clear the water from it."

Marnie knelt to the bottom, whipped her mask from her face, then put it back on. Lowering her head, she held the mask in place while she blew out through her nose. Tiny bubbles shot out of the valve in her mask and slowly the water left it.

It does all come back to you, she thought as she climbed out of the water for the second time. But then she felt weariness in every muscle and also remembered how tired she could be after diving.

Damon approached her and helped her take off her tank. "And now you think you're ready for the salvaging expedition?" Amusement laced his words.

With a wave of her hand, her back stiff with pride, she said, "Yes. I had no trouble remembering the correct procedures. As you can see, nothing went wrong." Then she sat in a lounge chair to remove her flippers.

"But then there are no dangers in the pool. Do you remember what to do if you foul? Or what to do if you're squeezed? Those things can happen to the best divers."

Marnie searched her memory. "Squeezing is when you descend too rapidly. It's when the pressure inside is greater than outside."

Damon stood above Marnie with his hands on his hips. "What do you do if this happens to you?"

"I have to make sure the pressure in my face mask is the same as on the outside. And don't descend faster than seventy-five feet per minute. I have to keep my ears cleared."

He nodded. "I'm impressed. You have an excellent memory. I still would like you to read up on the underwater emergency procedures in a pamphlet I have in my library. I'll give it to you to read today."

When the strength returned to her legs, Marnie rose and tensed then relaxed her muscles. "I'd like to use a tank off the coast here before we begin the salvage."

"That's an excellent idea. I'll go with you. You shouldn't dive alone."

Marnie looked at Damon through a curtain of lashes. "But won't you be busy getting everything ready for the expedition?"

He brushed the back of his hand across her cheek and said, "Now I can't go and have anything happen to my photographer, can I? What would I do then?" He smiled, a smile that melted Marnie's earlier resolve to only be civil to him.

She returned his smile, suddenly a thick silence between them. In the distance Marnie heard the shriek of the seabirds, the pounding of the surf against the rocks. But she was being drawn toward Damon, his gaze intense, dark with his emotions. Nothing existed but him.

They were only inches apart when a loud voice boomed, "Hello there, Damon. Glad to see you at home."

Damon muttered a curse beneath his breath and turned to watch a tall, lanky man approach them. A crooked grin appeared on the boyish face of the stranger as his blue eyes appraised Marnie.

"Hello. Who's this, old chap?" The stranger stuck his hand out for Marnie to shake.

Laughing, Marnie took the man's hand and shook it. "I'm Marnie Stevens."

"Marnie will be the photographer for my new book," Damon added, moving closer and draping an arm over her shoulder. "Marnie, this is Miles Whitman, a neighbor."

"It's nice to meet you, Mr. Whitman."

Two dimples broke the tan smoothness of Miles's cheeks as he smiled again. "Everyone calls me Miles, Marnie."

"What brings you over here so early, Miles? You never get up before noon." Damon began to walk toward the house.

"The news that you had a beautiful guest. The old grapevine is correct again."

"You mean James is still dating your housekeeper," Damon said.

With a sheepish grin on his face, Miles nodded. "In fact, this is her day off and I came to see if you would invite me to dinner."

Damon laughed, a robust laugh from deep in his throat. "Miles, you're the only person I know who has the nerve to invite himself to dinner. Yes, if you like conch salad and broiled red snapper."

"You bet. You know me. I'll eat anything that isn't moving. On second thought, if I'm hungry enough, I might eat something that moves."

With Damon's arm still on Marnie's shoulder, they entered the coolness of the house. A chill encased Marnie as a cold breeze from the air conditioner struck her wet bathing suit. Shivering, Marnie shrugged away from Damon.

"If you two will excuse me, I need to take a shower and change into some dry clothes." Marnie crossed the living room toward the foyer.

"Hurry back and I'll take you with me to the harbor. I need to check some things on my boat," Damon called out.

Marnie raced up the stairs two at a time. She peeled off her wet bathing suit and stepped into the shower. The warm spray of the water pounded her body. She felt refreshed as she left the shower and quickly

49

toweled herself dry. After dressing in a dust-blue halter top and matching shorts, she ran a brush through her wet hair and tied it back with a matching ribbon.

As she made her way downstairs, she heard Miles say, "Is she your newest conquest? She doesn't seem your type, old chap."

"For your information she is only my photographer for the salvage. That's all. She's pretty, but you're right. She's hardly my type."

"But I saw how close you two were by the pool. Not interested, you say?"

"It amuses me to flirt with her."

The muscles in Marnie's stomach tightened until they ached. She dug her nails into her palms in an effort to control herself, then made some noise in the foyer as she crossed it.

When she entered the living room, she strove to make her expression neutral while inside she seethed with rage. When she spoke, she kept her voice level, but it took all her strength to contain the trembling that threatened to seize her.

"I'm ready. I've been looking forward to seeing this island paradise." She forced herself to smile, but the corners of her mouth quivered from the strain.

Walking toward the front door, Damon asked, "Would you like to ride along, Miles?"

"No, not this time. All I care to see is my lounge chair by my pool. See you tonight." Miles waved as he jogged down the driveway.

"It's too bad he couldn't come with us. It would have been nice to have someone to talk with," Marnie said as she slid into the front seat of Damon's car.

Damon glanced sidelong at her but remained quiet as he shifted into first and pressed the accelerator. The wind blew strands of her hair behind her like golden ribbons dancing in the breeze. She leaned back and studied Damon through half-closed eyes.

She followed the line of his arrogantly set jaw down to the V-neck of his white sports shirt, stopping at the patch of black hair that covered his chest. The muscles of his chest were barely contained by the thin material of his shirt. She watched his shirt move with his even breathing, a half-smile curling his lips as he glanced at her and caught her gaze. Her cheeks reddening, she turned to examine the ocean beyond the road.

Hazy pools of heat simmered across the coastal highway. Tall Australian pines lined the road with aquamarine water peeking between the tall stately trees.

As they passed through Georgetown, Marnie exclaimed, "It's so small! There's only a few streets. And it seems like half of the buildings are banks. This is the capital?"

"There are only about fifteen thousand people that live on this island. This is all they need." There was a smile in his voice.

When Damon pulled into a parking space at the Georgetown harbor, Marnie breathed a sigh of relief. Sitting next to him in the car made her feel conscious again of how different this man was from her, of how rich and arrogant he was. *Nothing seems to bother him,* she thought. *He does what he pleases and doesn't take no for an answer.*

"I need to see the harbor master for a moment." Damon pointed toward a building. "If you like, go on down to the boat and look around. I'll be along in a while."

"Where's the boat?" But as she asked the question, Marnie saw a hundred-fifty-foot yacht painted white with navy-blue trim and knew that was it.

"There." He gestured toward the white yacht, then walked away, his strides brisk and long.

Marnie headed toward the yacht, its beautiful sleek lines a graceful work of art. Halfway down the pier, she surveyed the boat.

"It's a beauty, isn't it?" A deep voice sounded behind her.

Marnie twisted about to look at a short stocky man in his early sixties chewing on the end of an unlit pipe.

He limped down the pier toward her, scratching his gray beard and looking her over with a gleam in his brown eyes.

"I saw you with the boss. Do you want a tour?" The sound of his voice was a strange mixture of a Southern drawl with a Scottish lilt at the end of each sentence.

"She's a beauty. Do you stay on her?" Marnie asked as the old man helped her up on deck.

"I take care of her for the captain."

"Captain?"

"Mr. Wilson. He runs the boat when he's here. I'm the best tender around." He thrust his chest out and tapped it.

"Oh, then you're going on the salvage?"

"The captain couldn't do without me topside when the men are down yonder." The man leaned toward Marnie. "Do you know, little missy, that I saved the captain's life once when a school of sharks had him surrounded?"

"You did?" She smiled at the small man in front of her.

"Yep. He wouldn't be here today if it weren't for me. Why, if I hadn't kept my head on my shoulders, he would have been shark bait that day."

"Canie, I don't think you need to bore Miss Stevens with that story." Damon reclined against the railing and observed the two of them, his face lit with a smile, his eyes friendly.

Marnie tried to ignore the disconcerting directness of the look that he was studying her with, but she felt the warmth of Damon's gaze as it moved over her features. She wanted to turn and shout at him to quit toying with her but instead walked toward the door leading into the aft cabin and entered the cold interior.

She sensed Damon and Canie following her, then she heard Damon say, "Canie, you keep this place freezing. I don't understand why you picked to live in this hot, humid climate when you can't stand the heat."

"I couldn't leave the ocean. I was born here and have to be near it. What brought you down here, Captain?"

Marnie tuned them out as she scanned the salon with its navy-blue carpet and rust-colored chairs. She poked her head into the doorway of the galley and eating area, then descended the ladder to the lower deck, where she counted five bedrooms, all with double beds and a small bathroom. As she climbed back up to the top deck and started to step through the doorway to the salon, Damon blocked her way.

"How do you like her?" There was a caress in his question. He took her hand and pulled her through the doorway into the aft cabin.

Marnie glanced over Damon's shoulder to see where Canie was, but the cabin was empty. Looking back into Damon's face, she was drawn to his sensual mouth.

"She's nice, Damon."

She could smell his masculine cologne as he bent closer. Her breathing came in short gasps as his lips touched hers. He crushed her to him, his hard, lean strength molded against her as he stroked her back, massaging the tension from her. She wound her arms about his neck and clung to him. As his kiss deepened, a tingling sensation began deep within her to unfold and spread throughout her.

Then the words "It amuses me to flirt with her" echoed in her thoughts. They cut through the haze that shrouded her mind and penetrated her passion-drugged senses.

She tore herself from his grasp. "Don't you ever touch me again. I won't become one of your playthings, *Mr. Wilson.*" She breathed deeply to calm her galloping heartbeat. "You may think it's amusing to flirt with me, but *I don't.*"

Damon's eyes narrowed until they became slits. His jaw tightened; his body rigid. "So, you make it a habit to eavesdrop on my conversations?"

"You mean to tell me you didn't find that out in your report on me? I'm surprised. I was sure you'd have required a very thorough, detailed report. If I were you, I certainly would speak to my investigators the first chance I got."

Damon took first one step toward Marnie, then another.

"Don't come any closer."

He flexed his hands. "And why not, my dear?" Damon asked, now only a foot from her.

Marnie opened her mouth, but with lightning-quick speed his hand shot out and he dragged her to him. Damon smothered her words with the hard pressure of his mouth. As his kiss grew more intense, Marnie wanted to melt against him and return his hungry kiss.

I will not give in to him. I will not! she told herself, and stiffened against him.

Damon drew back and stared into her eyes. The air vibrated with tension, swirling with their warring emotions. Pushing her away, he pivoted.

Marnie watched his retreating figure. *It would be so easy to surrender.* She straightened. *But I'm here to do a job—and that is all.*

Chapter Four

Marnie leaned into the railing on the balcony as she absorbed the beauty of the pale blue sky with a silver shaft of sunlight streaking across the water. Marnie listened to the rhythmic sound of the surf, the whisper of the palm leaves. The light breeze stroked her, enveloping her in its silky warmth.

"It's something to see," Miles said as he walked up to Marnie and stood beside her. "There has never been a sunset quite as beautiful as those I see here on Grand Cayman."

Marnie watched the clouds swallow the orange-gold orb that hung suspended in the gray-blue sky and wanted this peaceful moment to continue, but with Miles's words the spell was broken. Turning, she offered him a smile.

"This whole island is like a drug. I feel dizzy from its beauty."

"It's kind of ruined my reputation of being a cynic.

But I felt the same way the first time I came to Grand Cayman." Miles drained his drink and placed it on a table.

"Do you scuba dive?" Marnie asked, and turned to look at the puffs of pink clouds floating above her.

He laughed. "Scuba dive! I can hardly swim. You wouldn't catch me in the ocean if my life depended on it."

"But with all this water, I thought surely you did. I just assumed . . ."

Miles stepped closer and whispered, "Marnie, let me give you a word of advice from an old cynic. Don't assume anything, especially in Damon's company. I've known that man for over ten years, and I believe you'd be safer using a bit of caution where he's concerned."

Marnie looked Miles straight in the eye and asked, "Why do you say that? He's just my employer for the next year. Nothing more, I assure you."

"I know what can happen when Damon turns on the old charm. All your well-intended wishes will fly out the window." Miles swept his arm in the direction of the ocean.

"You profess to be his friend and yet you stand here and warn me to be careful. You're the second person I know that has said that to me. Damon has no interest in me. He told you that himself."

Miles grinned, a crooked smile that brightened his features. "I *am* his friend. What I said to you doesn't change that. But Damon feels a need to show everyone he's above the rest of us mere mortals and that he doesn't need anyone—especially a lowly creature like a woman."

"Why does he feel that way?"

Miles shook his head slowly. "It was a long time ago, but I don't think he's ever forgotten Catherine." Moving closer, he leaned over as if to impart a secret. "If you knew about her, I think you'd understand him better."

"I hope I'm not interrupting anything," Damon said.

As Damon approached them, Marnie clamped her jaws together and gripped the railing. *Catherine?* Marnie shook the name from her thoughts as Damon halted near her—too near her.

"What has Miles been telling you? The island gossip?" Damon asked.

"Oh, nothing. I think I'll see if Mrs. Carson needs any help." She hurried toward the French doors before Damon said anything else.

Her pulse raced. A familiar tingling sensation teased her, urging her toward Damon. With a quickness of breath, she stood in the center of the living room, trying to calm the excitement that hammered in her veins. She saw herself clasped in Damon's arms on the yacht, his lips warm and soft as they traced the line of her jaw to her earlobe.

No, I can't be trapped in his snare! she whispered to herself, her heart fluttering. *Remember Robert and Anita. Do you want to be hurt again?* But in her mind's eye she followed the movement of Damon's lips as they nibbled her neck.

She shivered. *Stop it!* she told herself. The vision vanished, her legs suddenly weak. She fell into a chair, breathing deeply.

"Marnie, is everything all right? You look pale." Damon stood in the doorway to the terrace, his face masked by the shadows of evening.

"It's nothing," she murmured.

"Are you feeling well? Perhaps you got too much sun today." Advancing into the room, Damon halted in front of her and knelt. He took her hands within his and held them tightly. "Maybe I should help you to your room."

58

Marnie jerked her head up. "No!"

His concern trapped her. She felt herself being mesmerized by his gray eyes. Abruptly, she tore her hands from his grasp and scrambled to her feet.

"Leave me alone! I don't like you pretending concern where there is none. I'm fine." Marnie turned her back on him, her stance rigid. She was overpowered by a primitive force that drew her toward him, as if she were a meteor being pulled into the earth's gravity.

When he spoke, his hard tone cut through her. "I'm no different from anyone else. I eat, sleep, work like the next man. I care about someone in my employ if for no other reason than if you get sick that will delay the expedition."

Marnie's fingernails stabbed the palms of her hands and the hair on the nape of her neck rose as she sensed him moving behind her. He grabbed an arm and spun her around.

A shutter fell over his eyes. In a softer tone Damon said, "There's no reason why we can't be friends. We have to work closely together off and on for the next year. You'll be living in my house. I think we should call a truce. A deal?" He extended his hand for her to shake.

Marnie stared at the hand for a moment, then clasped it. "A deal."

"Now that that's settled, let's eat. It's been a long day and Mrs. Carson is an excellent cook." A smile touched his voice.

Marnie looked up and saw Miles in the doorway regarding them with an odd expression on his face.

Damon continued, "I think that's why Miles always seems to wander over here every Monday when his housekeeper has her day off." His eyes held a metallic gleam as he regarded her. He cupped her elbow and guided her toward the dining room.

When they entered the dining room, Damon pulled Marnie's chair out for her. She sat down and surveyed the elegantly set table with sparkling Waterford crystal and delicately painted bone china. After Damon was seated at the other end of the table, Mrs. Carson served a tureen of clam chowder. Marnie dipped her spoon into the thick whitish soup and tasted it.

"Mmm. My mother would love this recipe, Mrs. Carson," Marnie said, then sipped another spoonful of the chowder. "She loves seafood and is always looking for different recipes."

"I'll write it down for you so you can send it to her," Mrs. Carson said, then set the tureen in the middle of the table.

When Mrs. Carson served the conch salad, Marnie said, "I've never had conch in a salad."

"You'd better get used to it. It's one of the favorite dishes of the island," Miles said.

Marnie sampled the salad. "It's delicious."

"If you like, when we dive tomorrow we can get some conch. I thought I'd take my spear gun and catch some fish," Damon said.

"Will we have time to do all that?" Marnie took another bite of her salad.

"We can make time." Damon smiled at her.

During the main course the conversation turned to the salvage. A bright look of excitement softened Damon's dark features and his voice had a silky quality to it.

"Do you have the crew ready for Wednesday?" Miles asked. "I heard Toothless hasn't returned from his fishing expedition to Cayman Brac."

"He'll be at the boat Wednesday morning before everyone else. I'd wait for him, though, if he didn't show up. He's the best diver in these islands." Damon relaxed in his chair and took a sip of his coffee.

"Toothless? That's an odd name." Marnie finished her broiled red snapper and wiped her mouth with her napkin.

"That's because he doesn't have a tooth in his mouth. He hates wearing his dentures, so most of the time he doesn't," Damon answered.

"But how does he eat?" Marnie asked, trying to imagine a man without teeth eating corn on the cob.

"Oh, he manages quite well," Miles said.

Marnie shook her head when Damon started to refill her coffee cup. "Who else is going to be on the dive with you besides Toothless?"

"His partner, Mickey Edwards, Canie, you, and four crewmen to help Canie with the boat."

"Only two divers?" Marnie asked.

Damon leveled a penetrating look at her. "You forget that I'll dive also. When we find the wreck and start salvaging, I'll have to bring in more equipment like an airlift. Then I'll use more divers. Until then we'll work in two teams. Mickey and Toothless. You and me." His intense gaze made a swift appraisal of her, finally resting on her mouth. A slow smile crept across his features, a smile filled with his compelling masculinity.

You and me. The words vibrated in her mind. Marnie looked at her empty coffee cup. "I think I'll have some more coffee."

After he finished pouring the coffee, Damon looked up into her dark eyes. "Does diving alone with me frighten you?"

Marnie saw the amusement that danced in his eyes and retorted, "Certainly not!" She took a sip of her coffee, the steaming brew burning her lips.

"Have I upset you, Marnie?" Damon arched a brow. His gray eyes sparkled as the corners of his mouth twitched with his suppressed laughter.

The color in her cheeks deepened until Marnie was sure they were as red as the fish they had just eaten. When Miles came to her rescue with a question, she drew in a relieved breath.

"Damon, other people have thought they knew the location of that sunken Spanish galleon. What makes you think *you* are going to find it?"

"I've done some extensive research and plotted its course to that day that the hurricane struck it. I have a pretty good idea where it went down from the data I gathered at the archives in Seville."

"Then I'm wishing you success. Good luck, old chap. You'll need it. Searching for a sunken ship is like searching for a needle in a haystack. Near to impossible, Damon."

"But *not* impossible. Spanish galleons are located all the time."

"Usually by accident," Miles said.

When Mrs. Carson entered the dining room again, carrying a silver tray, Damon said, "In your honor, Marnie, Mrs. Carson made her best dessert—Cherries Jubilee."

Marnie smiled at the housekeeper. "Thank you."

Mrs. Carson laid the tray before Damon, who withdrew some matches from his pocket. As Mrs. Carson quietly left the room, she turned the lights off, casting the room in a silver glow from the moonlight that flowed through the large window overlooking the ocean. When Damon lit the dessert, a burst of flames consumed the brandy. Marnie looked into Damon's intense gray eyes, each appraising the other, the glow of the flames making Damon's features seem demonic.

When the flames died down, Marnie dragged her gaze from his and said, "I'll turn on the lights." She was on her feet before anyone could say anything across the room.

As Damon dished up the dessert, Marnie asked Miles, "This island seems so different from other places in the Caribbean. If you had one day, where would you go sight-seeing first?"

Miles cocked his head and stared off into space for a few minutes before he answered. "Well, I guess the Sea Turtle Farm is a must for a tourist. Then there are the bat caves around the south end of the island that interest some people."

Marnie shivered. "I think I'll forget about the caves. Bats aren't my favorite creatures. But the turtle farm sounds interesting."

"And don't forget the blowholes at the east end," Damon said, handing a plate to Marnie and Miles.

"Blowholes?" Marnie asked.

"It's a place offshore where water spouts like a whale. Actually all they are are the openings to subterranean passages. When high tide occurs, the waves rush in and water shoots into the air." Damon took a bite of his dessert.

"There's no way I can see all of the island in one day and dive in the morning."

"Well, I'll be glad to give you a grand tour of the island," Miles said.

"I'm afraid she won't be able to take you up on that invitation, Miles," Damon interrupted, his voice suddenly brisk, formal.

"Why not, Damon?"

"Because in the morning you'll be busy with your diving lesson . . ."

"And in the afternoon?" Marnie felt her temper rising.

"You'll be busy, too." His tone dismissed the subject, but Marnie didn't feel like heeding the warning.

"Doing what, Mr. Wilson?"

"I hired you to do a job. I don't need to explain every

minute to you. You'll be working tomorrow. That's final." Damon rose.

"I think it's late. I'll be leaving. Thanks for the dinner, Damon." Miles stood and offered Marnie one of his crooked grins before he headed for the door.

When Marnie heard the front door close, she directed all of her defiance at Damon, both of them staring at the other over the expanse of the dining room table, each with eyes narrow and gaze unwavering.

Between clenched teeth Marnie said, "Doing what? I have a right to know."

"I'm warning you. I don't like being questioned constantly. I'm paying you well to do a job." His voice struck her like a physical blow.

Marnie shrank back, drew in a deep breath, and said, "You couldn't pay me enough to follow your orders without question, Mr. Wilson."

Damon advanced toward her, his eyes bright, as Marnie stepped back.

"Everyone has his price. Money is a very powerful weapon." He held out his hand, palm flat. "I have your future in my hand. I have many powerful friends, Marnie. I could easily destroy all of your hopes." He moved his fingers slowly and stiffly inward.

Marnie watched wide-eyed until his hand was a tight ball, then she looked him in the eye. "Why? Why are you doing this to me? What pleasure do you get by playing your little games, Damon?" she whispered in a husky voice. A knot formed in her throat, and she swallowed past the lump as she examined the disturbing intensity of his granite features.

A strange emotion flickered across his face before Damon quickly masked his expression. *Regret? No, this man doesn't regret what he does,* Marnie thought, and turned to escape the now too warm room.

Damon grasped her by the arm and turned her to

face him. As he stroked the crease of anger on her forehead, trying to smooth it away, he eased the crush on her arm and looked into her eyes.

Sighing, Damon said, "Okay. If you must know, Marnie, I don't think it's wise for you to get involved with Miles."

"Involved! I have no intention of becoming involved with *any man.* He's your friend. Why do you say that about him?"

"He may be my neighbor, but I also know that Miles is a playboy of the worst kind." Damon's eyes took on a strange glint.

"Can you say you're any better?" Marnie whispered the question so low she was afraid Damon didn't hear her.

"We'll dive in the morning, then I'll take you to the turtle farm tomorrow afternoon."

"Do I get a choice in the matter?"

Damon raised a brow. "Which would you rather do? Work with me or see the island—with me?"

Marnie sighed. "See the island."

"See. I know your mind better than you do."

"You only think you do. When you give a girl such an unattractive choice, what do you think she's going to say?"

He tapped his finger to his temple. "That's the key to my success with the ladies." He leaned closer and whispered, "But don't give my secret away."

Laughter bubbled from Marnie's throat. "I may use it to blackmail you later when I want something."

Damon's features became mockingly serious. "You stoop to blackmail! Never! You're too nice a girl."

Anita's accusation leaped into her thoughts. *You were always the good little girl.* Marnie frowned.

Being the good little girl doesn't always pay off, Marnie said to herself.

Damon increased the pressure on her arm. "No more frowns tonight. I won't allow it. I know what we'll do. I'll show you the blowholes tonight."

"In the dark?"

With a glance out the window, Damon said, "The moon is full and will give off enough light for you to see them. Get a sweater and let's go."

Marnie hesitated, thinking of the romantic setting that the moonlight could create on the beach. *Should I go?* she asked herself as she studied Damon.

"That's an order, Miss Stevens," he said in a stern voice, but his eyes gleamed with amusement.

She stood at attention. "Yes, sir."

Marnie banished her doubts to the dark recesses of her mind and hurried upstairs. Grabbing her white sweater, she headed back down the stairs. *Quit trying to read something into everything he does,* she thought.

When Marnie stopped in front of Damon, he reached for her hand. "Let's go. The high tide is coming in."

Marnie rested her head on the back of the car seat and let the breeze play with her hair. The cool wind felt good on her hot cheeks. Damon pressed the accelerator to the floor and the car sped down the highway that cut across the island. As Damon slowed the Mercedes to a respectable speed, he turned left onto the coastal highway.

Bringing the coupe to a halt on the side of the road near the beach, Damon hopped out of the car and hurried around the back of it to open Marnie's door.

As Marnie climbed out, she exclaimed, "Such a gentleman."

Damon bowed deeply, sweeping his arm across his body. "Anything for a beautiful lady. Once in a great while my manners slip through the barrier I place around them and show themselves. You'd better take advantage of them while they're here. Never know

66

when they will leave." He captured her hand in his grasp and pulled her along behind him across the rocky terrain toward the water.

"Hold it." Marnie tugged on Damon's hand.

He stopped and glanced at her, his brows lifting in a silent question.

"I'm getting sand in my shoes. Let me take them off."

He bowed again. "No, fair lady. Your knight in shining armor is here to do your bidding. Let me."

When Damon's fingers touched the flesh of her ankle to unbuckle her shoe, a bolt of searing pleasure spread up her leg and radiated throughout her body. Slowly he slid the shoe from her foot, his fingers caressing her flesh. He repeated the action with the other foot. When he looked up she wanted to run her fingers through his black hair. His hypnotic gaze captured hers. The silver rays of the moonlight softened his features as he rose and gathered her into his embrace.

Her breathing came in short, shallow gasps as his lips played havoc with her senses. Damon bit teasingly at her neck before his lips trailed burning kisses to her mouth. He traced the outline of her mouth with his tongue, then pressed his lips against hers. His hand slipped under her blouse and stroked her flesh before unhooking her bra. His fiery touch sent flames raging through her body. As hard as she tried, she couldn't summon any resistance.

Cupping a breast, he massaged it with a circular motion of his thumb. The word *No* seeped into Marnie's thoughts, but all she wanted now was his mouth to claim hers again in a passionate union. He nibbled the tip of her ear, teasing her with the flick of his tongue until Marnie moaned and pulled his head around, his lips brushing hers. Damon kissed her on the mouth, a kiss that drew the last of her doubts from her mind. Melting against him, Marnie returned his kiss, wanting to surrender completely to him.

But the brightness of a car's headlights bathed them and Damon pulled away, staring down at her for a brief moment as the car rounded the bend and sped past them on the coastal highway. The moonlight threw his features into the shadows and she tried to read his expression but couldn't. Damon stood away from her and faced the ocean.

Finally, when Marnie's breathing returned to normal, she broke the silence. "Where—where are the blowholes?" Her heart was still pounding against her breasts, her blood racing through her veins.

Silence.

In the moonlight Marnie saw his ramrod straight body as he looked at the water. He balled his hands at his sides, then released the fists.

"Damon." His name was a whisper.

He turned and said, "Out there," his tone putting a distance between them as he pointed to the left.

Marnie's gaze traced the direction of his arm and saw the spouts of water shooting straight up in the air. The spraying seawater seemed like diamond droplets pelting the ocean as they fell back down into it. She stared at the blowholes until she sensed Damon turn to leave.

"It's getting late. We have a lot to do tomorrow. I want to start early," he called over his shoulder as he made his way toward the car.

Marnie followed, opened her own door, and then climbed into the seat, avoiding a glance at Damon. The blood pounded against her forehead, making her head ache from tension. She rubbed her temples, but still her head throbbed.

The car moved forward and Damon made a U turn in the road. As he raced the car along the darkened road toward the villa, the only sounds Marnie heard were the roar of the engine and the surf breaking against the reef.

When Damon screeched the car to a halt on the deserted road, Marnie was thrown forward, Damon's arm shooting out to stop her from hitting the dashboard.

"What's wrong?" Marnie asked.

He gestured toward the road and Marnie saw a huge gray crab lumbering across the pavement. The crab froze in the glare of the headlights. His claws, a foot apart, were as large as a man's hands, open and ready to grip onto something. He stood with his body raised off the road staring at them.

"What's he doing this far from the water?" Marnie asked.

"He's called the gray land crab and is seen rarely in the daylight. Want to get a better look at him?"

Marnie shook her head. "I've never seen a crab so big. Those claws look ferocious."

"They are. I have heard of them biting through a tire wall. You shouldn't get too close to them." Damon put the car into first and skirted the crab.

And I shouldn't get too close to you, Marnie thought.

Chapter Five

"We can swim out to the reef. The marine life is abundant on it. And you can practice ditching while you're down. You never know when you'll be required to take a tank off someone and replace it with another set. When we reach the reef and I give you the signal"—Damon stuck his thumbs up—"I want you to take off your breathing set, surface, then dive back down and put your tank on. Think you can do it?"

"Yes." Marnie squinted her eyes and looked across the water toward the reef. "Is it very deep?"

"No. About fifteen or twenty feet where we're going. Ready?"

Marnie nodded, then adjusted her face mask to the right position. She took heavy steps to the edge of the water and glanced over at Damon before she entered, the warm water soothing her tense muscles. *Relax*, she thought. *You'll do everything all right.*

Kicking her feet and keeping her hands at her sides, Marnie swam a little behind Damon to the reef. With each breath she took she felt more relaxed until her breathing came in an even, normal pace, her movements one fluid motion.

As they swam, suspended over the reef, Damon signaled to her to dive to the bottom and ditch her breathing apparatus. She scanned the fish-infested water, then headed for the bottom. When Marnie touched the sand with her flippers, she knelt and unsnapped the straps holding her tank in place. Taking one final breath from her mouthpiece, she swam for the surface, releasing her breath slowly as she headed for the top. Breaking surface, Marnie sucked in a large gulp of air, then duck-dived toward the bottom. When she reached her tank, she took a deep breath from her mouthpiece, then strapped on her tank. She glanced up once and noticed Damon hovering over her, watching her every move.

Damon signaled her with the okay sign, and she nodded as she took in breaths and released them. *I did it,* she thought. A calm settled over her as he motioned for her to follow him. They began to circle the area. Marnie watched a school of small fish striped black, white, and yellow dart away as she neared them. A beautiful blue queen angelfish with a yellow crown came near her and inspected her before swimming away. The fan-shaped coral swayed with the current while vivid colored fish nibbled on the surfaces of the rock formations and beneath the elkhorn coral.

Marnie was observing a butterfly fish when Damon tugged on her arm and pointed to the side of him, where, a few feet away, there was a three-foot-long moray eel with its mouth open, its razor-sharp teeth visible. Moving away from the eel, Damon pointed to a

71

school of yellow grunts under a massive tangle of staghorn coral. All of a sudden, the fish fled, and a few seconds later Marnie saw the reason—a barracuda.

As long as Damon's here, I'm safe, she thought.

Then suddenly the barracuda swam straight for them. Marnie tensed; her breathing became labored. After the barracuda circled them a few times, it swam away. Marnie trembled with relief as she watched the silver fish disappear.

Checking his pressure gauge, Damon pointed toward the surface. While they were heading for shore, Marnie shivered as she thought of the four-foot-long barracuda charging toward them. *It was only curious,* she told herself, but she still couldn't forget its fierce-looking face.

Marnie surfaced in waist-high water, spat her mouthpiece out, and lifted the mask from her face. Taking her flippers off, she trudged from the water, fell to her knees, and sucked air into her lungs. Exhaustion made her legs feel like lead.

When Damon emerged from the sea and lay beside her, she looked over at him and offered a faint smile. "I'd forgotten how wonderful diving could be. Invigorating, but exhausting," she said.

"You won't have any problem. Here, let me help you off with your tank. It's got to be heavy now that we're on land again."

Marnie knelt in the sand and allowed Damon to unstrap her tank as she licked the salt off her lips. "Am I thirsty! You didn't by any chance bring something to drink, did you? My mouth feels like it's stuffed with cotton."

"Better than that. I brought a picnic lunch for us. I'd thought about going back out and spearfishing, but obviously that barracuda has staked his territory."

Marnie twisted around and smiled. "He can have all the fish he wants on that reef. You can't argue with a barracuda." There was laughter mixed with her words. "Here, let me help you with your tank."

After they had divested themselves of their diving gear, they sat on the beach and stared out across the blue expanse of water. The sun glistened on the surface like thousands of diamonds scattered in a field, the water looking almost white.

Marnie brushed the sand off her hands and legs. "I think one of the things I like the best about this island is that you can find an isolated spot. So many places this beautiful are jammed with tourists, trashing the beaches and water. I hope this place never becomes famous."

"When that happens I'll move on. There's a peaceful, soothing quality about Grand Cayman that draws me back here every few months."

Damon pushed himself to his feet and extended his hand to Marnie. "Enough beauty for one day. Let's eat. I've worked up a gigantic appetite. How about you?"

"If a shark leaped out of the picnic basket, I think I'd eat it."

Damon tilted his head to one side and combed his fingers through his damp curls. "It seems I remember you telling me once that you like to eat a big lunch. Well, I hope Mrs. Carson packed enough for two, or you might starve." A lazy, wicked look crept over his features as he dusted off the sand.

"You *would* eat the whole lunch without a second thought."

He said, "You bet," then made a mad dash for the car.

Marnie raced after him, laughter overcoming her halfway across the beach, and she sank to the sand, laughing. When she looked up at Damon, he was lounging against the car door with his arms and legs crossed.

"Do I have to bring the picnic to you, or do you think you can manage the few remaining yards to those trees?" Amusement rang deep in his voice.

Marnie followed the direction of his gesture and saw a group of Australian pines clustered along the beach, their wispy branches catching the light breeze.

"I think I can manage if you promise me some refreshment for my effort."

Damon rummaged through the basket and said, "And entertainment. Wait till you see my juggling act with these oranges."

"That I can wait to see. I need something to eat before I watch you juggle. I might not have enough strength to laugh." Walking to the basket, Marnie opened it to peek inside. "Roasted chicken, breadfruit puffs, and fruit salad. That should take care of me. What are you going to eat?" She turned to look at him.

Damon lay down on the blanket, clasped his hands behind his head, and stared back at her—the picture of relaxation.

A warmth encircled her throat. In the distance she heard the waves lapping the shore, the seabirds screeching, the whistle of the breeze through the trees. But time seemed to stand still for Marnie as she looked into Damon's eyes.

"You have a very kissable mouth, Marnie," he whispered as he reached up and drew her toward him.

Her heart skipped a beat when their lips were only an inch apart, so close that their breaths tangled. It seemed like an eternity before his mouth touched hers, nibbling her lips until Marnie thought she would faint from the teasing. She buried her hands in the soft curls of his hair and pulled him closer, his lips taking hers completely now.

Damon covered her body with his, one of his hands traveling down a strap of her bathing suit to the V of her neckline. He slipped his hand under the bathing suit and caressed a breast. Shivers shot down her spine as his hand massaged her hip with slow, hypnotic strokes. His mouth descended slowly as if Damon wanted to savor the minute before possession as long as possible. Finally his mouth opened over hers, claiming her lips in a hungry, demanding kiss that sent an avalanche of swirling sensations snowballing through her. An intoxicating breathlessness seized her lungs at his fresh male scent that mingled with the tang of the sea.

A noise penetrated Marnie's drugged mind. She tore her mouth from Damon's and pushed at him. "Someone's coming."

Slowly he lifted his head and stared across the sand. "Damn it!" He sat up and busied himself preparing lunch.

Covering her cheeks with her hands, she turned away from Damon. The heat of her blush seared her fingertips. A group of people piled out of a car and headed along the beach away from them. When the group had disappeared from view, Marnie twisted about and looked at Damon. Her gaze caught his, but the magic of moments before was gone. A mask of indifference had replaced the look of desire that had been in the circles of slate gray.

He handed her a plate of food, saying, "Here."

Marnie looked at the food and suddenly was no longer hungry. Her stomach churned with her boiling emotions. *How can he be so unaffected by what just happened between us?* she wondered. *Am I just another conquest to add to his long list?*

Confused, she took the plate from Damon and laid it on the blanket beside her, then picked up a glass and said, "I would like some tea, please."

As Damon poured the drink into her glass, he ignored her questioning look. *How can he kiss me so passionately one minute and be so in control of himself the next?* she asked herself, her body trembling from the emotions that he had stirred. Marnie sipped her tea and nibbled on a breadfruit puff. *Well, whatever game he's playing, I'm not going to be a participant,* she vowed silently.

When she placed her half-empty plate down, Damon said, "I thought you were hungry. Mrs. Carson will be disappointed that you didn't touch the roasted chicken."

"I've lost my appetite," she fired back at him in a harsher voice than she had intended.

"You're too skinny as it is. I hope I don't find you refusing to eat whenever something goes wrong."

His retort caused a pallor to steal into her cheeks as Marnie stared at him. "You have no right to criticize me. It's you who gets so angry when something goes wrong. You can't accept the word *no*. You have to bully people until you get your way, Mr. Wilson." Words tumbled out of her mouth as she vented her anger at him. She hated him for being so cool and self-assured while inside her feelings were swirling from the intense emotions that his kisses had created. It was a game to him, something to pass the time, while to her it had been deadly serious. And that's what frightened her the most—the feelings he provoked in her that she wanted left buried.

"Was I bullying you a moment ago, Marnie?"

His question was spoken so softly that she had to bend forward to hear it, but she heard the steeliness in the question and her control snapped. Rage trembled through her and she exploded. "Why you . . ."

He crushed her to him and the grinding pressure of his mouth smothered any words she was going to say. He parted her lips, the kiss demanding a response as passion flared between them like a brushfire. Her earlier emotions flooded her senses, leaving her feeling warm, contented as his lips pressed into hers. Her senses tried to dominate her mind, but she fought the passionate feeling that was enveloping her and struggled to remain in control.

Wedging her arms between them, Marnie pushed away from him and stood on trembling legs, ignoring the ardent look that was chiseled in his features. Instead she headed down the beach, driving herself on until, exhausted, she could no longer place one foot in front of the other. She sank to the sand and stared at the water.

"I hate him," she whispered to herself. "I feel like I'm losing all my self-control. All he has to do is kiss me and I seem to . . ."

Her thoughts were disrupted as a shadow fell across her. When she looked up into Damon's face, Marnie knew she was helpless to fight that primitive longing that possessed her when he touched her.

He held out his hand for her and said, "It's time we go, Marnie. I want you to see the turtle farm." His voice held no emotion nor did his expression.

Marnie ignored his extended hand and scrambled to her feet. After she brushed the sand from her, she walked to the car and slipped on her red shorts and shirt over her dry bathing suit then put on her sandals.

In silence they drove to the turtle farm, Marnie keeping her eyes on the road ahead. When they entered the farm, she walked in front of Damon. Passing rows of tanks filled with year-old green sea turtles, Marnie slowed her pace and glanced toward Damon. With his jaw tightly clamped shut, he stared at a tank with giant sea turtles in it. One huge turtle surfaced and eyed Damon and Marnie before submerging to the bottom again with a splash.

Marnie followed Damon down the long row of tanks where the loggerheads, hawksbills, and ridleys were kept for observation.

"This farm has been here since nineteen sixty-eight and recently has become self-sufficient, its own captive adult breeding turtles laying all the eggs it needs." Damon took Marnie's hand, the touch warm to her cold fingers. "Come. I'll show you the baby turtles. They immediately take the eggs that are laid on their artificial beaches and put them into the hatchery, where the babies' rate of survival is much higher than in the wild. As you know, turtle meat is quite a popular dish on the island, but they do return some of the turtles they raise to the sea. Still, the primary function of the farm is to raise turtles for their delicious meat."

Marnie scanned the artificial beach area, aware of Damon's intense gaze upon her. Damon's stare made Marnie uncomfortable. She tugged her hand from his and without waiting for him proceeded toward the area where the babies were kept.

For a long moment Marnie watched hundreds of baby turtles clambering to get out and poking their heads above the water. She tensed when Damon placed a hand on her shoulder.

"About this afternoon at the picnic, Marnie. I didn't . . ."

Marnie shrugged away from Damon and turned to face him. "No, Damon, I'm aware of your reputation and I'm a grown woman." Her anger gnawed at her stomach. "Don't worry about me. This afternoon meant nothing."

Marnie had started to walk away when Damon grabbed her arm and spun her around. "I started to say before you so rudely interrupted me that I didn't mean to come on so strongly, that I'm sorry."

Marnie planted a hand on her waist and moved back a step. "My, Mr. Wilson, it comes as a surprise and a shock that you'd concern yourself with anyone else's feelings but your own," she said, speaking in a voice strained with emotion.

"Shh." Stepping closer, Damon tossed his head in the direction of a couple walking near them. "It's time we go. I have to visit Amy in the hospital."

On the ride through the West End Marnie studied the passing scenery, taking in the small homes with banana, papaya, and mango trees in their front yards. They passed through Georgetown and stopped in front of the hospital, not a word spoken the whole trip.

As Damon turned the ignition off, he said, "I'll only be a few minutes," and reached to open the car door.

Marnie placed her hand on the doorknob. "May I come with you?"

"If you want."

When Damon and Marnie entered the hospital room, Amy, a petite child of eight, threw herself into Damon's arms before he was halfway into the room.

"Oh, Auntie told me you were coming, Damon!" The girl's pretty face split with a grin. "This is the most beautiful doll I could ever own." Amy held the baby doll up for Damon and Marnie to see, then cradled it to her. "Thank you, Damon, for bringing it back from the States. I'm never going to let it go." Amy squeezed the doll tighter.

Damon smiled, a smile that brightened his whole

face, that made him seem years younger than thirty-three. "Then how am I going to get those hugs and kisses that I've been waiting for and counting on?"

Amy cocked her head to one side and looked at Damon. Then suddenly she tossed the doll onto the bed and hurled herself into Damon's arms again. He whirled her around, then gently laid her on the bed.

"You need your rest, young lady. I think you've had enough excitement for one day. Amy, I want you to meet a friend of mine. This is Marnie Stevens from the United States."

Amy offered Marnie a brilliant smile, a startling contrast against her sallow complexion. "Is Damon your boyfriend?" Amy blurted out, looking from Damon to Marnie. "Auntie says you need a wife." With a question in her eyes Amy raised an eyebrow at Damon.

Marnie swallowed hard and murmured, "Damon and I are just friends. I'm going to help him with the salvage."

"Oh, I'd hoped I could be your flower girl at your wedding. I've always wanted to be one." Amy's smile dissolved into a pout.

Damon sat on the bed and held Amy's hand in his. "Amy, when I do get married, you'll be the first one I ask to be my flower girl. The only one. I won't have anyone but you." Bending over, he kissed her on the cheek. "We have to be going, Princess. But I'll be back to see you soon." He rose and grasped Marnie's hand in a tight grip.

"Amy, I hope you'll let me come back and see you, too," Marnie said.

The little girl's face beamed. "Oh, yes. I love to have visitors—especially Damon."

When they left the room, Damon dropped Marnie's

hand and turned away. He stood motionless in the hallway, his back to her.

Sensing something was wrong, Marnie touched him on the arm and said, "Amy's really sick, isn't she?" When Marnie received no answer, she stood in front of Damon and saw his eyes dark with emotion, the clenched jaw that etched his face in pain.

"Yes. She's dying. She was putting on an act for me. She always does and I go along with it. But with each visit it becomes harder for me to act my part." Pain laced each of his words. He took a step forward, slow and rigid.

"Can't anything be done?"

"No. I've tried everything money can buy. But the doctors say she won't live. It's only a matter of time."

An uneasy silence fell over them on the ride to the villa. Marnie felt the agony that played across Damon's features and longed to smooth the hurt that lined his brow, but he had retreated into a stony shell and she didn't know how to penetrate it. *He really cares about Amy,* she thought. *Like the children at the orphanage.*

"Damon, I'm sorry about Amy." She laid a hand on his arm. "I know it must hurt . . ."

"Does it give you satisfaction to find out I have a heart that bleeds like everyone else's?" He shot her a slicing look, then turned to study the road ahead.

"Oh! Why do you always misread my intention?"

He remained silent, concentrating on the road.

When they arrived at the villa, Marnie, without looking at Damon, said, "Thank you for taking me to see the turtle farm." But when she placed her hand on the door release, Damon reached over and pulled her hand away.

"I want you to be ready in an hour to go out to dinner. This is Mrs. Carson's day off."

"I really don't feel like eating. I'll just make a sandwich and eat in my room." Suddenly all the weariness of the day's activities invaded Marnie.

"You forget that I'm the fella that can't take no for an answer. Be ready in an hour. *I am* taking you to this restaurant I want you to see." He reached across her lap and opened the door, then straightened to wait for her to leave.

Marnie studied his solemn features. *What's the use in arguing?* she thought. *I am hungry.*

She climbed out of the car and closed the door. She felt Damon's gaze follow her movements and lifted her chin a fraction. *He won't rattle me,* she repeated to herself as she walked across the driveway and entered the house without a backward glance.

When she shut the door to her bedroom, she collapsed onto the bed and lay still for several minutes, listening to the quiet of the house, waiting for any sounds that meant he was near.

Marnie rolled over onto her back and stared at the ceiling. She glanced at her watch and knew she had to get ready soon or be late. A smile curled her lips as she decided to nap just for a while, her eyes drooping closed . . .

Marnie felt her body being lifted and shaken. She heard a voice, as if the person was shouting at her through a long tunnel. "Get up, Marnie. We're going to be late."

She combed her fingers through her hair and slowly rolled her head from side to side. "Robert?" Marnie mumbled, her mind clouded with sleep.

She blinked her eyes and tried to focus on the face that loomed before hers and bit by bit the features were arranged into a familiar pattern.

"No, I'm not Robert!"

"Damon! What are you doing in my apartment?" Struggling to sit up in bed, Marnie scanned the room, her brows furrowed. Then she remembered where she was.

Damon moved off the bed and stood staring down at her with a dark expression on his face. "If you aren't dressed in fifteen minutes and downstairs, I'll dress you myself." He turned and strode from the room.

When the sound of the door slamming shut finished vibrating throughout the room, Marnie slipped her feet to the floor and walked into the bathroom. She undressed and turned the water on in the bathtub.

"Well, I'm going to have a bath and wash the sand off whether you like it or not, Mr. Wilson," she said aloud, and stepped into the cool water to quickly wash the dirt from her.

After toweling dry, Marnie jammed her arms into the sleeves of a robe and belted it. She hurried into the bedroom and was moving toward the closet when she froze, her eyes dilated. She brought a hand up to stifle a cry. Her scream knifed the air.

When the door burst open and Damon demanded, "What's wrong?" Marnie pointed and laughed.

"Sorry, Damon. I just didn't expect my visitor." A gray lizard clung to a wall near her bed, issuing a loud, "Gecko, gecko!"

Damon laughed and walked to the wall where the lizard sat observing them with large eyes. "Occasionally one gets into the house."

Plucking the lizard from the wall, Damon crossed the room to the sliding glass door and placed the lizard on the balcony. The gecko looked up at Damon, then scurried away.

"That was a pretty ferocious-looking creature. I've never been crazy about lizards," Marnie said.

With four long strides Damon was standing in front of her. Her heartbeat began its mad pace as he took her hand.

"You're trembling, Marnie."

Damon trailed a finger down her jaw. "I'd never let anything hurt you while you're under my care." His voice was strangely gentle, soft.

It's you who scares me, Marnie thought. *I've never felt this way before.*

Damon's gaze traveled from her eyes to her mouth, then to the hollow at the base of her throat. Suddenly she felt very vulnerable with only a terry cloth bathrobe on and this man inches from her. Forcing her hand from his grasp, she backed away from him.

"If you'll give me ten more minutes, I'll be ready."

"I'll be downstairs waiting." Damon left, glancing back before shutting the door, his gaze taking in her uncombed hair, her bare feet, and the robe she wore.

Dressed in black satin pants with a white silk blouse that had flounces down the front, Marnie sat and slipped her feet into strapless white high heels, then stood and surveyed herself in the full-length mirror on the bathroom door. She ran a brush through her damp golden curls, applied some lipstick, and walked from the room.

She caught sight of Damon below in the hallway and stopped at the top of the stairs. He stood straight and proud with his white slacks and navy-blue sports jacket that fitted his build snugly, outlining his powerful muscles. Marnie stared at his full lips and remembered the burning kisses that had sought to possess her. *And almost succeeded,* she thought.

Damon looked up, brushed a dark curl from his forehead, and smiled. Marnie felt the warmth flow from his eyes and envelop her. She gripped the banister and slowly descended the stairs. Their gazes locked in an embrace. Marnie ran her tongue over her lips and looked beyond him, breaking the hold he had over her.

"Where are we going to eat?" she asked.

"The Grand Old House. The food is excellent as well as the atmosphere."

Damon took Marnie's hand and led her to his car. On the twenty-minute drive across the island Marnie watched the sky turn from a dark gray to the black of night. No longer could she see the ocean beyond the road. Only an occasional house or village lighted the way.

When Marnie entered the Grand Old House, she fell in love with it immediately. "It's charming, Damon." She surveyed the turn-of-the-century house with its ceiling fans, hanging brass pots, elegantly set tables, and screened-in veranda. A gentle breeze from the beach blew through the room.

After they were seated on the veranda, Marnie studied the many entrees, then looked up and asked, "What do you suggest, Damon? There are so many unusual dishes."

He glanced up from his menu, an amused smile tugging at the corners of his mouth. "If you like, I'll order for you."

Marnie nodded and laid her menu to the side.

When the waiter appeared, Damon said, "We will both have a spinach salad, stuffed mushrooms, and the turtle steak."

"Would you care to order a drink, sir?" the waiter asked.

Damon raised a brow in a question to Marnie, and she shook her head.

"No, but I'd like a bottle of white wine with our dinner."

"Thank you, sir." The waiter wrote the order on his pad, then left.

Marnie sipped her water and scanned the veranda, the smells of the different dishes tantalizing her. It was as if everything were slowed down, the pace unhurried as the waiters served the diners in a relaxed atmosphere. Marnie leaned back and let the tension-free surroundings seep into her soul, drawing the tautness from her.

Damon was staring at her as she looked at him, his gaze mentally dissecting her. The look he sent her had a devastating effect on her senses, the silence growing between them, the tenseness returning.

"Why do you want to salvage the *Santa Santiago?*" She blurted the question out when she could no longer stand the silence.

"I love history. The *Santa Santiago* is history. There is a fortune in mercury on the ship, but what I'm really interested in is the artifacts we'll find telling us about the people that were coming to the New World." His eyes turned a dark gray with a silver gleam in their depths. "The *Santa Santiago* left Spain traveling for Veracruz, Mexico, but the galleon never reached its destination. People's whole lives were on that ship—all their possessions. I want to find out about those people to write about them. There were over five hundred people on that ship."

She sensed the thirst for knowledge conveyed in every word he spoke. *I, too, search for that knowledge —with my camera,* she thought. Suddenly she felt very close to Damon.

"But once you find this galleon, how will you salvage it? Won't it be buried under tons of sand?" Doubt sounded in her voice, mingled with the hope that the expedition would succeed.

"Not all of it will be buried, I hope. The removing of the sand deck by deck is what takes so long. But it'll be worth it!" Damon paused as the waiter served them their stuffed mushrooms.

"When we find the wreck, we'll use airlifts to remove the sand, then we'll slowly sift through the sand and debris for any artifacts. The time required will depend on how much of the ship is above the sand."

"How many divers will you hire?" Marnie asked, then took a bite of a mushroom, the dish teasing her palate with its delicious taste.

A smile rested on his features as he spoke. "I'm not sure until I see the condition of the wreck. The salvage divers will have to work two weeks on, two weeks off. So I'll have to hire enough for two crews."

Marnie stared at him. "How about me, Damon? How long do I work? Is it still going to be a year of my time?"

Marnie held her breath as the silence replaced his reply. It was as if everyone in the room was waiting for his answer.

"You'll stay as long as it's necessary for the job to be completed. I told you the salvage may last a year, so it might be a year of your time, Marnie."

"Damon, at the beginning I thought this job was for only a few months. I have other commitments."

She clamped her teeth together until her jaw hurt. *A year in Damon's company*, she thought. *How will I survive being so close to him all day long—all night long—and not end up hurt?*

Chapter Six

Marnie felt the vibrations of the engines as Canie started them. Toothless and Mickey Edwards untied the ropes on the pier then hopped aboard as the yacht slipped out of its berth. Toothless neatly wound the rope and laid it on the deck.

She noticed that Toothless not only didn't have any teeth but was bald as well, his head tanned from the sun and glistening with sweat. The man lifted several tanks at one time, the muscles bulging in his huge arms.

"Toothless saved my life once by lifting a boulder from my leg while we were diving. Thank God, he's as strong as a bull."

Marnie turned at the sound of the strange voice and nodded to Mickey Edwards. "Toothless is one of the largest men I've ever seen. All muscles."

"I agree, and not only strong but intelligent as well. Toothless is an unusual man." Mickey stuck his hand out and shook Marnie's. "I'm Mickey Edwards, Toothless's partner."

"I know. Damon told me. I'm Marnie Stevens, the photographer."

He flashed her a boyish grin. "I know. Damon told me."

They both laughed.

"Mickey!" Damon called out.

As Marnie and Mickey twisted about to see Damon approaching them, Mickey whispered, "Well, I guess I'd better earn my pay. I'm sure glad I like to dive, or I'd find it hard making a living. Work isn't one of the thrills of my life."

"We need to check the diving equipment," Damon said in a businesslike tone. "And I suggest, Miss Stevens, you check your equipment, too."

"I have everything ready," Marnie replied, her heartbeat increasing at the sight of Damon.

"I hope you do," Damon said over his shoulder as he and Mickey walked toward the stern of the yacht where Toothless was working.

Marnie followed the movements of Mickey with her eyes and relaxed the frown on her face. *I like Mickey,* she thought. Of average height, Mickey was very different from Damon. Where Damon had black hair, Mickey's was blond. Mickey's eyes were bright with merriment—brown twinkling eyes that made her feel that she had known him for years. Marnie's thoughts flew back to her childhood and she remembered wishing for a brother to protect her the way her best friend's brother had.

"Like Mickey," she whispered, and felt she had found an ally against Damon. She clenched the railing. "Someone to help me fight these feelings."

As her heartbeat slowed to a normal rate, she

loosened her grip on the railing and stared across the crystal-clear water at the fading shoreline of Grand Cayman. When the last bit of land vanished from her sight, Marnie turned to make her way to her cabin, but stopped abruptly when she saw Damon standing quietly a few feet from her.

"Is the equipment in order?" she finally asked when she could no longer tolerate the silence that electrified the air. She dropped her gaze to the water, avoiding his searching look.

"Yes. Are your quarters okay?" He moved to stand beside her at the railing, his arm touching hers.

"Yes."

"I believe you're the luckiest person on this boat," he said.

Marnie sensed him appraising her and continued to stare at the white, frothing foam that the yacht made as it glided through the water. "Why do you say that?"

"Because you don't have to share a cabin with Canie. Perhaps you would like to move your things into my cabin and let Canie have one by himself. He's the loudest snorer I've ever heard. No one on this boat will escape hearing him at night. But worst of all me."

Marnie heard the light tone of his voice, but she knew under all of his teasing he was serious about sharing a cabin. She forced her own voice to be light as she said, "I really feel for you, but we all have to make sacrifices for this expedition."

"And what is your sacrifice, Marnie?"

"Being near you, putting up with your arrogance," she said, and turned to walk away.

She listened to his roar of laughter as she made her way to the aft cabin. Again her heartbeat pulsated blood rapidly through her body. She sought the quiet of her quarters, the safety of the locked door.

Marnie lay on the bed and stared at the ceiling. Her

sleepless night had left her tired with memories of the reason she had tossed and turned most of the night flooding her mind.

"Why can't I get him out of my mind? When I'm around him, I tremble inside. When I'm away from him, he fills my every thought," she said aloud to the silent cabin. "Why do I want to end up hurt again?"

As she pondered the question, the movement of the yacht lulled her to sleep. . . .

"Marnie! Marnie, open this door *now!*"

Marnie shook her head to rid herself of the web of sleep that still clung to her mind. As a loud pounding penetrated her thoughts, Marnie scurried off the bed and across the cabin to open the door.

"Yes?" She yawned and looked up into Damon's scowling face.

"I was about to break the door down. What took you so long? I've been standing here ten minutes trying to get your attention."

"Well, you have my attention now. What do you want, Damon?" Marnie tried to make her voice sound bored.

"It's almost dinnertime and you're supposed to fix it."

Marnie's eyes widened. "That's news to me. Since when did you hire me as the cook?"

"Everyone takes his turn cooking and cleaning up the dishes. We all drew straws and you won. You're the lucky person to cook for the next three days."

Anger coursed through her veins as she clenched her jaw and said, "I don't like being excluded from things like that. Are you sure this isn't a way for you to get me to do all the cooking and cleaning for the expedition? After all, I'm just a female and hardly good for anything other than that."

Damon seized her arm, his fingers pressing into her

flesh for a brief moment before he let her go, and said in a voice that held his temper in check, "Women are good for more than cooking and cleaning. Share my cabin and I'll teach you what else—that is, if you can learn." Turning, he strode away, glancing over his shoulder at the end of the passageway and ordering, "Be in the galley in ten minutes. We're all hungry, and we don't like to wait."

Marnie hit the door with her fist. Pain spread from her hand up her arm. She rubbed her bruised knuckles and slammed the door to her cabin.

"That man!"

Marnie looked at her wrinkled cotton dress and strode to her suitcases on the floor by the bed. She snapped one open and withdrew a pair of shorts and a halter top that covered just the necessities. A devilish grin appeared on her face as she took off her dress and flung it on the floor. After she donned the peach-colored shorts and matching top, she ran a brush quickly through her hair, put on some lipstick, and left the cabin.

With light, bouncy steps Marnie headed for the galley. *I'll fix you dinner, Damon Wilson. One you won't forget,* she said to herself, and entered the kitchen. With a narrowed gaze she scanned the room, then stood in front of the refrigerator and opened it. She studied the contents, her brow wrinkled in deep thought.

"Hello. May I be of some help?" Mickey's kind voice interrupted her.

Marnie pushed the door closed and smiled up at him. "Yes. I'm a terrible cook. Any suggestions for dinner?"

Mickey swung his arm from behind him. He was holding two big, fat groupers on the end of a line. "Why don't you let me pan fry this fish for our dinner? I just caught it. It'll sure beat eating canned meat."

"You're an answer to a girl's prayers, Mickey. That sounds great." She flattened herself against the refrigerator and swept her arm across her body. "Right this way, sir. I'll prepare mashed potatoes and a salad. I suppose we'd better enjoy the fresh greens while we can."

As Mickey searched the cabinets for a frying pan, he said, "Damon will probably fly to Grand Cayman once a week. We won't be far off the coast of Little Cayman." When he found the pan, he pulled it out. "So I hope he'll bring some things back for us like fresh vegetables and fruit."

After peeling the potatoes, Marnie cut them up into small chunks, heaped them into a large pot and placed it on the stove. "I didn't know he would be leaving every week."

"Damon is a busy man. He still runs Eastern Communications, so he has to check in with his office in New York from time to time."

"But he told me that he spent his time writing books, that he didn't care about the company." Marnie stopped rinsing the lettuce and looked at Mickey.

"Could you ever see Damon turning the control of his business completely over to anybody? He's not that type of man. Yes, writing is his first love, but he can't forget his responsibilities to his family."

"Family?"

"His mother is still alive and lives near New York City with Damon's younger sister."

"Oh," Marnie mumbled, and turned the water back on to continue washing the lettuce.

I don't know anything about Damon, she said to herself. *He has a family and I thought he was alone. Why? Because in all the time we have spent together this last week he has never mentioned his family.* She stared at the torn bits of lettuce. *Why do I want to know more about him? He's just my boss.*

Marnie looked sidelong at Mickey as he cut into the fish. "How did you get to know a man like Damon Wilson?"

Mickey looked up from placing a fillet into the hot oil. As the sizzling sound filled the small galley, he grinned and said, "Toothless taught Damon to dive years ago. Toothless introduced us when I dropped out of college a few years back and moved here. They've dived together in these waters for quite some time." He turned back and put another piece of fish into the pan. "So when Damon wanted to locate the *Santa Santiago,* he asked us to help him."

"Miles Whitman said that finding this ship will be like finding a needle in a haystack. Will it be that hard?" Marnie asked.

Mickey laughed, a deep throaty laugh. "Yes, it'll be hard. Miles always has had a way of describing a problem quite accurately. We have a depth-sounding device on the boat that'll tell us when we've run over something that's different from the ocean floor. And we have a magnetometer that'll tell us if there is any unusual mass of iron on the bottom, such as the cannons of a galleon. Those instruments will help us to locate that needle."

"If you happen to run over the ship."

"We will. Now you'd better round up everyone for dinner, Marnie. The fish is nearly cooked."

Marnie mashed the potatoes then set the table. After she was sure everything was ready, she walked through the salon onto the deck at the stern, where Damon was staring at the wake of the boat.

"Damon," she called softly.

He stood still, not turning and acknowledging he had

heard her, so she said louder, "Damon. Dinner is ready."

Damon whirled and faced her. "Oh, it's you. What did you say?"

"Dinner is ready."

"I'll be in in a while."

With hands planted on her waist, Marnie tapped her foot and in a stern voice said, "Mr. Wilson, dinner is ready now. You made me get up to fix this dinner and you'll eat it while it's hot."

She glared at him while a parade of emotions flashed across his features. Finally amusement settled on his face.

"Are you giving me orders, Captain?" Damon asked, laughter filling his voice.

"You can decide what you think I was doing while walking into the cabin. I want you in the galley in five minutes with your hands washed and you ready to eat a good dinner." She spun on her heel and headed for the door.

"Could you wait to walk with me?" came the quiet question as she placed her hand on the doorknob.

She sensed him behind her and tensed. He reached around her and opened the door. Their hands touched briefly, chills flashing up her arm.

"I don't know how the mashed potatoes and salad will be, but I know Mickey can fry the best grouper in the islands," Damon said.

Arching a brow, Marnie turned and looked at Damon. His voice held a sharp edge to it, but his expression was impassive.

When Marnie and Damon entered the room everyone but Canie and Don, one of the crewmen, was seated at the table. Marnie smiled at Mickey, then sat next to him while Damon sat opposite her at the oblong table.

Marnie took a bite of the grouper and the fish melted in her mouth. She savored the delicious-tasting fish with each bite.

When the meal was finished, she leaned toward Mickey and whispered, "Damon said you can fix the best grouper in these islands and I believe him. That was wonderful! Any night I'm making dinner feel free to fish."

A brilliant smile spread across Mickey's features. "Ma'am, any time I can accommodate you, I will." He rose and started to gather up the plates.

"Mickey, I would like to see you now. Let Marnie clean up this mess." Damon gestured toward the dirty plates and glasses.

"I'll be with you in a minute. I'm going to help Marnie clear off this table." Mickey sent Damon a sharp look, then resumed gathering up the plates.

Damon stared at Marnie with an angry glint in his gray eyes before walking from the room.

She released a sigh of relief. "Mickey, please let me finish this. You've helped me enough already. I'm quite capable of handling the dishes without you." With a quick glance at the door Damon had just walked through, Marnie turned back to Mickey. "I don't want to cause any trouble between you two." She touched Mickey's arm. "Put those down and I'll see you later."

"We should be stopping for the night soon. Damon wants to drop anchor off the shore of Little Cayman. Walk with me on the deck when you're finished."

"That's a deal." Marnie watched Mickey stroll from the galley. After he left, Marnie turned and looked at the pile of dirty dishes that were stacked in the sink. She blew out a breath of air and began washing the dishes.

Halfway through the cleanup the yacht stopped and

the roar of the engines died. Marnie looked out the porthole and saw the faraway lights of Little Cayman, the darkened outline of the island on the horizon.

"Can I have some of that grouper? I hope you all saved some for me and Don. He'll be along in a while." Canie stood in the doorway, his unlit pipe stuck between his teeth.

"Sure. I put some away just for you. Have a seat and I'll fix a plate." Marnie busied herself preparing the leftovers for Canie.

At the sound of a motorboat speeding away from the yacht, Marnie glanced up and shot Canie a questioning look.

"That's Mickey leaving for Little Cayman. Some piece of equipment needs to be replaced, so he's flying to Grand Cayman to pick it up. Be back before morning I 'spect." Canie dug into the food placed before him. "I sure do work up an appetite when I'm at sea. Must be the salt air that does it to me."

Marnie tuned Canie out and listened to the distant rumble of the motorboat, the sound finally fading. *Well, I guess I'll take that walk by myself,* she thought. She felt angry and disappointed at the same time. *He didn't tell me he was going. Men!*

Marnie quickly finished the dishes and said, "When you're through, just put your plate in the sink. I'll clean it later, Canie."

"Don't worry. I can clean one little old plate and glass."

The cool breeze from the water enveloped Marnie when she stepped out onto the deck. Trailing a finger along the railing, she headed for the bow. As she stared at the full moon, clouds drifted across the path of its rays as they fell on the sea. She turned and searched the distant shoreline for the motorboat and saw its silhouette against the water, a dark shadow speeding toward the island, the glittering water spreading out in all directions from it.

"I'm sorry I ruined your little party tonight, Marnie. Mickey asked me to tell you he'd see you tomorrow morning."

Marnie didn't turn when she heard Damon's voice, a voice that held no regrets. The peacefulness that surrounded her shattered and flew away as if a sea gull had swooped down and taken it for its meal.

"Marnie?" That soft, gentle voice of his spoke this time.

"I would like to be alone, Damon."

He was beside her now, stroking her arm. "What's wrong? Perhaps I can help."

She wanted to shout, "You," but instead remained quiet, very conscious of his fingers caressing her flesh.

"Tomorrow we begin the search when Mickey comes back." He broke into the silence that filled the night air. "I have made you angry. I'm sorry for that."

She rounded on him. "But not for sending Mickey away." She felt as if her eyes were piercing his flesh with daggers.

He stared down at her, his finger tracing her jaw, leaving a warm path where it had been. "No, I'm not sorry that Mickey *had* to go. I wanted to talk with you and to . . ." His voice faded into silence.

"Do what?" She tilted her head back to try to read the expression in his eyes, but they were shrouded in the shadows.

"This." His lips touched hers in a whisper, the kiss deepening as he hugged her to him. "And this." His mouth traveled over her features, caressing each with the feather-light touch of his lips.

He pulled away when Marnie thought she would drown in the delicious sensations he evoked within her.

"Mmm. You taste definitely salty," Damon murmured against the softness of her hair.

She pressed closer and listened to his uneven breathing, his chest rapidly rising and falling. She smiled in the dark, glad of the effect she had on him.

"Right now there are no disappointments to face—only the hope that we'll find the ship immediately. This is the best time—before you have started a project and you still have all your dreams about it."

She moved from his embrace and searched his features. "But surely when you find the ship—that will be the best moment of the expedition. Then your dreams will be met."

He turned and stared at the water below. "Perhaps. But what if the ship doesn't live up to my dreams? Then it will be a disappointment. No, I think I enjoy this moment the most, right before everything begins." Damon reached out and drew Marnie into the circle of his arms. "It's nice to share this moment with someone that I like."

"There are moments when I'm not so sure you like me."

"You doubt *me!*"

"Yes. Damon Wilson, you're a man of mystery. I know little about you really. Only what I read in the newspapers and on the backs of your books."

"Ask me anything. I'll tell you all about myself."

She gathered her courage and asked, "Who's Catherine?"

Damon stiffened, then dropped his hands from her waist. The playful smile vanished as he twisted away from her.

"Why do you want to know about *her?*" His voice sounded savage, a strange huskiness within it, his features sculpted in cold marble.

"Miles told me I might understand you better if I

knew about her. But if you don't want to tell me, that's fine. It's really rather late and I think I'll go to bed." She began to walk away.

"No!"

Marnie froze, then slowly turned and stood motionless as she waited for him to speak.

"I told you I would tell you about myself and I will. Catherine was a woman that I loved a long time ago. She was older than I by five years, but when you're nineteen nothing seems to matter. The world is yours to take and enjoy, or so I thought."

Marnie wanted to press her fingers across his mouth to stop his next words.

"Catherine was the most beautiful woman I had ever seen. Her hair was silver, her eyes cinnamon. When she entered a room, everyone's gaze followed her movements, so powerful was her femininity. And so shallow her loyalty and worth as a human being." The last sentence was part laughter, part bitterness. He pivoted and stared at the water.

"It's a long story and a long time ago. I won't bore you with the details. The ending is all that matters. She married my father after shattering my belief in the female race and destroying my parent's marriage. You see, my father had more to offer her than I, a young kid who pleased her in bed, as she put it, but who wasn't powerful and wealthy enough for her. I've long gotten over the blow to my pride." He waved his arm in the air as if to dismiss the memory.

Marnie touched Damon's arm hesitantly at first, then with more boldness she grasped it. "I'm sorry. But all women aren't like that, Damon."

He whirled and faced her. "I've seen women flock to me now that I'm rich, powerful. I have a lot to offer them. Of course, I always had my share before, but then I was a Wilson, the heir to my father's kingdom.

Catherine drove my father to an early grave. Dad committed suicide, leaving her a rich widow. Now she's married to another rich older man, spending his money like it's going out of style."

Words of comfort formed in Marnie's mind, but as she stared at his strained features, she couldn't say them.

"Now you know. Is your curiosity appeased, Marnie?" His question struck her.

She shrank back, shaking her head. "I'm sorry. I didn't mean to drag up painful memories. If I had known . . ."

"You wouldn't have asked me." He smiled and presented his back to her. "I think it's time you did go to bed. Tomorrow is a big day."

"Damon."

"Go!"

Marnie stared a moment at his back, then turned and left the deck. When she was inside the quiet of her cabin, she collapsed against the closed door and shuddered.

"Oh, Damon. I *am* sorry," Marnie whispered, but she remembered his unmoving back and knew she had overstepped her bounds.

Chapter Seven

Marnie settled into the seat and waited for the plane to take off. "It's nice to put my feet on solid ground again." The plane began to pick up speed for its takeoff.

"I wouldn't say this was solid ground, but I think you'll enjoy being on Grand Cayman once more, even if it's only for the day." Damon watched her out of the corner of his eye.

"I just wish we had found the wreckage by now. Moving in slow circles in the water day after day isn't very exciting." She sent him an enticing smile.

He chuckled. "And I thought *I* was impatient. We've only been searching for a week. I would have been surprised if we had found it that fast, but I don't think it will be much longer. In fact, when we return this evening, they may have good news for us."

Marnie looked at Damon and whispered, "I hope so."

A silver gleam appeared deep within his eyes, pulling her toward him. She looked away from him and inspected the sea below them.

"We're almost there. I can see Grand Cayman." Marnie gestured toward the window.

"Have you made sure you have enough film for the next several weeks?"

"Yes, of course."

"I like the pictures you've taken so far. They're good."

"Thank you," Marnie murmured as the plane started its descent, and she tensed and tried to prepare herself for the landing.

Damon squeezed her hand. "Relax." His hand covered hers in gentle reassurance.

Marnie leaned back as the plane's wheels locked into place and touched down on the ground.

After they left the plane, Damon guided her toward his car. "I'll have to stop by the bank first," he said, and opened the door for her.

Marnie remained standing while Damon rounded the car and opened his own door. "This feels good after the boat and plane ride. I don't know how sailors can stay out for months and not feel like their legs aren't their own. To have the floor always moving—no thanks for me."

As Damon started the car, a smile registered on his dark compelling features. "I was going to ask you to run away with me and live with me on the seven seas in my boat." Damon arranged his features into an exaggerated frown. "Oh, well. I'll just have to find some other lucky creature to share my boat with."

"Me and my big mouth." She snapped her fingers. "I missed my lucky chance." Marnie glanced at Damon's frown, then burst out laughing when she could no longer restrain herself.

Damon threw her a shocked look, his eyes wide. He brought the car to a halt at the side of the road and said in a very serious voice, "You laugh at me?"

Marnie tried to contain her laughter as she looked up into his sparkling eyes, but when she saw the corners of his mouth quiver from suppressing his own laughter, hers increased. Tears rolled down her cheeks. She dashed them away as Damon joined her in laughing.

When they had composed themselves enough for Damon to continue driving, he said, "I needed to laugh, Marnie. It's been a long time since I've laughed that much. Thanks."

He sent Marnie a look that warmed her. A slow blush covered her cheeks as she turned to stare out the window. *There I go again—blushing every time he looks at me,* she thought. She tried to control the color that heightened her cheeks, but her face felt hot beneath her fingertips as she remembered the look he gave her, a very male look filled with desire.

Damon maneuvered the car into a parking space near the Barclays Bank International in Georgetown. "I won't be too long. Shop while I'm in the bank and I'll meet you here in an hour. Then we can visit Amy at the hospital before having lunch at a quaint little restaurant I know in Hell."

"Hell!"

Damon laughed. "Yes, there's a town on Grand Cayman called Hell. A lot of people that visit here have their letters postmarked from Hell. The lady that runs the post office is kept quite busy."

"Perhaps I should spend my time writing a letter. I'm sure my mother would love getting a letter from me from Hell."

As he stood next to the car, he said, "See you in an hour and . . ."

"And don't be late," Marnie interrupted, mimicking his deep serious voice.

"No, I was going to say don't spend all your money, but don't be late isn't bad advice, because I might just leave you here."

"And have Canie take all the pictures you need with his little old camera?"

Damon scratched his head. "Mmm. That's not a bad idea. Now why didn't I think of that from the beginning? It certainly would have saved me a lot of trouble putting up with you."

Marnie scrambled out of the car and faced Damon in mocked indignation. "You wouldn't dare replace the most valuable member of your expedition!" She planted her hands on her waist and stared up at him. "Who's going to record for all the world to see that beautiful treasure you're going to find?"

Damon raised a brow. "How about Toothless?"

Marnie spun around and walked toward the sidewalk. She threw him a look over her shoulder as she said, "I won't even dignify that question with an answer. I'll just be here in one hour and you'd better be here, too, sir." A grin slipped through the pout on her lips and her eyes twinkled as she watched him move toward the bank.

Marnie began her leisurely walk toward the sea, inspecting the shop windows on her way and stopping once to cool off in a store. At the end of Cardinal Avenue she stared at the sparkling water, the refreshing coolness beckoning her. A deep sigh escaped her lips as she turned the corner.

On Fort Street Marnie glanced at a jewelry store display window and saw a pair of black coral cuff links the color of Damon's hair. On impulse she turned back and walked into the shop.

After Marnie stepped into the air-conditioned interior of the jewelry store, she scanned the glass cabinets in the window until she saw the cuff links.

"May I see those, please?" Marnie asked the salesgirl. When Marnie touched the cuff links, she knew they were perfect for Damon. "I'll take them."

Marnie felt silly buying Damon the cuff links. *He has hundreds of pairs, I'm sure,* she told herself, but each time she looked at them she felt compelled to get them for him.

The salesgirl wrapped them up and gave Marnie the box. After paying for them, Marnie glanced at her watch and saw she had five minutes to get back to the car. She put the box into her white purse and hurried from the coolness of the store. Panting, she reached the car as Damon emerged from the bank. She leaned against it and tried to catch her breath.

"I was just about to give up hope that you'd be on time." Damon climbed into the Mercedes.

"I'm on time."

Damon inspected his watch. "You're exactly two minutes and twenty seconds late. Try to do better next time, madame."

Marnie bowed. "Oh, please, forgive me for the transgression. My life would be worthless without your pardon."

Damon flipped his hand toward her. "Get in and I'll consider your request." His gaze flickered over her, taking in her flushed cheeks and windblown hair.

"You must have run from the other end of town. What did you do with your time, Marnie Stevens?"

"I was searching for a gift." Marnie dug into her purse, withdrew the box, and held the wrapped present out for him. "Open it. It's for you."

With brows raised, he stared wide-eyed at the gift.

"For me!" His fingers touched the box hesitantly. "Why, Marnie? It isn't my birthday."

Marnie thrust the present at him. "Because I wanted to, that's why, Damon Wilson. I saw these in a store window and they cried out to me to buy them for you."

Damon carefully peeled the wrapping paper away, then lifted the lid of the box. When he saw the black coral cuff links his face registered surprise. He fingered one, then looked up at Marnie.

His gray eyes were intense with a strange emotion deep within them, and in a husky voice he said, "Thank you, Marnie." He leaned across the seat and brushed his lips over hers. "Not many people give me presents. They usually expect ones from me. It's nice for a change to be on the other end."

Marnie felt flustered. She straightened in her seat and said, "Well, it's about time someone gave the boss a present." Marnie avoided Damon's gaze and added, "I'm starved. Show me the place that's so special before I faint from lack of food. If you remember correctly, you practically dragged me away from the breakfast table this morning." The words tumbled from Marnie's mouth—anything to fill the void between them.

"First, I want to visit Amy," he said.

When Damon started the car and pulled out into the stream of traffic, Marnie relaxed, no longer feeling the almost physical possession of Damon's gaze, weaving its magic over her, binding her to him.

In a few minutes they were at the hospital, Marnie's heart constricting at the sight of Amy, the girl's features listless as she lay in her bed.

"She wasn't expecting us," Damon whispered, and gripped Marnie's hand. He fought to keep the smile on his face, but his fingers dug into her flesh.

Damon walked to the bed and kissed Amy on the forehead. The girl's eyes fluttered open and she smiled, a faint wisp of a smile.

"Oh, Damon." Amy threw her arms around him and hugged him. "I'm so glad you came back. Auntie told me about your boat trip."

"Look who I brought to see you. Marnie." Damon pulled Marnie forward.

Amy's smile widened as she struggled to sit up while Damon propped the bed up for her and helped make her comfortable.

"Auntie says you take pretty pictures."

"Yes. If you like, I'll send you some of the wreck when we find it," Marnie said.

"Oh, please! I love to swim and snorkel. There are so many beautiful fish to look at along the reefs."

A nurse appeared in the doorway. "You all will have to leave now. Amy needs her rest."

Damon kissed Amy, then Marnie bent and kissed the little girl's cheek.

"I'll see you later, Princess," Damon said at the door as Amy closed her eyes.

Throughout the drive along the Seven Mile Beach Marnie half listened to Damon as he pointed out places of interest. Her mind drifted from Amy fighting to put up a brave front for everyone to the events of the last week on the yacht. She went over in her mind each day and still couldn't understand why Damon had been so kind to her since that first disastrous day.

She smiled as she remembered the second night that she had fixed dinner and how Damon had helped her in the kitchen with the meal and the cleanup. Their laughter had filled the galley when they had gotten into a water fight and she had ended it by throwing up her arms in defeat. *What a mess,* she thought.

The motion of the car coming to a stop brought

Marnie out of her musing. She surveyed the restaurant sitting on the beach—a two-story building made of stone—before she climbed from the car.

Damon took her elbow and led her toward the restaurant. "Spanish Bay Reef has a wonderful buffet on their terrace overlooking the water."

When they walked through the buffet line, Marnie piled her plate high with different kinds of fish, lobster, corn on the cob, and salad.

Damon scooped up a cakelike dish with spinach in the middle and said, "Try this Turtle Florentine. It's delicious. You like the turtle steak. You'll like this, too."

Marnie sat at a picnic table and eyed her Turtle Florentine.

Laughing, Damon said, "Go ahead. Try it."

"Are you sure it's good?" Marnie asked, wrinkling her nose as she cut her fork into it.

"Yes, Marnie. Didn't I tell you once I wouldn't let anything harm you?" He watched her intently as she lifted the fork to her mouth.

The dish dissolved on her tongue, the spicy tang of the meat tantalizing. "It's good! I'll never doubt your word again. I never thought when I came to Grand Cayman that I'd eat turtle, but they have so many wonderful dishes with it." Marnie took another bite, the aroma of the different kinds of food teasing her senses as their odors drifted to her nose.

When the meal was over, Marnie leaned back on the bench and laid her hand on her waist. "I couldn't eat another bite. I don't think I'll have to dive with weights for a week with all the food I've eaten here today. If I went into the water right now, I'd go straight to the bottom."

Laugh lines appeared at the corners of Damon's eyes as he smiled. "Let's walk along the beach and work off some of that meal. I'll have you into shape in no time, Marnie."

"Oh, you're a slave driver, Damon Wilson. How long a walk am I in for?" She slanted a look at him through lowered lashes.

"I have a place in mind where it's quiet and we can walk for, say, a mile."

"A mile! I didn't eat that much! Let's compromise. A half of a mile?"

His smile widened. "We'll see."

Marnie slipped her feet out of her sandals and wiggled her toes in the fine white sand, then tossed her sandals into the car and took Damon's hand. She peered around him and asked, "What do you have under your arm?"

"I thought you might like a siesta after gorging yourself at the restaurant."

"I didn't see you picking at your food either. At least *I* didn't go back for *seconds.*"

"You got me there. I brought a hammock for you and one for me so we can sleep—if that's what you would like to do, Marnie." His gray eyes gleamed.

"Mmm—sleeping sounds great. When do we have to be at the airport?"

"In four hours. We have lots of time to enjoy ourselves." Damon stopped at one palm tree and looped the rope around its trunk.

"You don't have any more business to conduct today?"

"Nope. I'm a fast worker when I want to be. I couldn't see working all day while the sun was out." When he was through securing the hammock, he helped Marnie into it. "I'll awaken you in an hour so we can go for that walk."

Marnie smiled as he turned from her and walked to a

palm tree not far from her. She watched him fix his hammock, then climb into it, before she turned to look out across the emerald green water, the waves lapping the beach, a rhythmic sound that lured Marnie toward drowsiness. Her eyelids became heavier and heavier until the last thing she remembered hearing was the sound of the surf breaking over the sand.

A gentle nudge pulled her up toward the brightness, her eyes heavily veiled. With a mist still clinging to her mind, Marnie stared up at Damon leaning over her with a sensual expression etched into his features. Opening her arms wide, Marnie drew Damon to her. She kissed him, her senses swimming in a delicious pool of sleepiness that mingled with her passion. He pulled away, his tongue tracing the outline of her mouth in exquisite delight until she craved him with an ache that intensified with each brush of his lips against her flesh. Then his mouth captured hers again, and pleasure erupted deep within her, so intense a feeling that her breath was driven from her lungs, her heart pounding with her desire for him. She tightened her hold on Damon and felt herself being pulled rapidly toward a mind-shattering sensation.

Then suddenly Damon tore himself from her embrace and straightened. While Marnie struggled to regain control of her senses, Damon's gaze swept over her once before he turned and strode away.

Marnie touched her bruised lips and stared at Damon's retreating figure. *Why, Damon? Was I getting too close?* she asked herself, the memory of his kisses overpowering her, drugging her senses.

Her gaze followed his movements as he walked along the beach, his hands thrust into his pants' pockets, his stride stiff. He kicked at something, then turned and stared at the water. Marnie couldn't read his expression, but she sensed his conflicting feelings.

She swung her legs to the sand and pushed herself to a standing position, then headed in the opposite direction from Damon, too confused to face him, too hurt to see his rejection of her in his face.

I threw myself at him like so many other women have. Marnie walked along the water, letting the warmth of it caress her feet. *But I can't deny it any longer,* she thought. *I love him!*

"It's useless, though. He can't love me. I'm not sure he can love anyone after Catherine," Marnie whispered, her soft words caught by the breeze and whisked away. "He must never know how I feel. I can't tell him." She lifted her chin and squared her shoulders. "I won't walk away from this salvage with nothing left. I can at least keep my self-respect." She turned and strode toward the car.

Damon was waiting for her, a neutral expression on his face with a touch of reserve in his gray eyes as if he had come to a decision. Sitting next to him, she sensed the invisible wall between them and without a word stared out the window as he started the car.

They sped toward the airport, the silence eating at her nerves until she thought she would scream from the tension. She dug her fingernails into her palms and concentrated on the pain that emanated from her hands.

"Good morning, Canie. I didn't see you when Damon and I got back last night. Any luck yesterday?" Marnie extended her arms above her head and bent backward to stretch her muscles.

"Nope, little missy. The only good thing is we searched a section we won't search again. We'll move on today and hope we're lucky. Maybe the ship was wrecked down in this area." Canie pointed toward the bow of the boat.

"Later this morning I want to take some pictures of you working the sonar device. After breakfast I'll bring my camera around and get a shot or two of you steering the yacht, too."

Marnie flashed Canie a smile as she walked to the stern and he began to head for the bow. She listened for Canie to start the engines, to hear their familiar hum, to feel the yacht move forward.

This is my favorite time of day, she thought as she stared at the orange ribbon streaking the eastern sky. The velvet black of the heavens was turning a smoky color as the bright light of the sun peeked over the horizon. The world stirred and awoke as Marnie stood leaning against the railing and watched the sun rise, the sky changing from a thin orange strand to a golden brilliance.

"I missed you yesterday. The boat was pretty lonely without your voice to listen to or your face to watch." Mickey laid a hand on Marnie's shoulder and pressed his fingers into her skin. "Did you enjoy your visit to Grand Cayman?"

Marnie continued to stare at the water washed in silver tones as the sun's rays glittered off its surface. "Yes. I liked Grand Cayman." She blocked from her thoughts the scene between her and Damon on the beach. The memory hurt too much.

"I hope we find this galleon soon. I'm not used to sitting around waiting. Reading, relaxing, and watching are all right on land, but I want to start some serious diving soon." Mickey turned Marnie around to look at him. "Do you want me to pose for some more pictures?" He flexed the muscles in his arms. "I'm not a bad model."

Marnie chuckled at Mickey's muscle-man pose. "I think I have all the shots I need of the equipment and the procedures for keeping it in order. Thanks, but

113

Damon seems satisfied with what I have already taken. I hope we find the ship soon, too."

"I put on the coffee. Would you like a cup?" Mickey asked, taking her hand.

"Yes. I've always liked sitting at the kitchen table at home and reading the paper leisurely before the day starts. I don't like to rush the beginning of the day or I never quite feel right during the rest of it."

As they sat at the table in the galley and sipped their coffee, Marnie listened to the creaking of the yacht as it moved through the water. *Will we find the galleon today?* she wondered.

"You have to give me a chance to win at gin rummy today. I'm already in the hole by a few hundred points," Mickey said, interrupting her thoughts.

Marnie grinned. "Five hundred twenty points, to be exact, but then who's keeping score?"

"I think you're a card shark disguised as a lady photographer."

"I'll give you the chance to lose more to me if that's what you want. At a penny a point it will take quite a lot of playing to win enough money to retire on."

"Well, it looks like we might have the time." Mickey lifted the coffeepot to fill Marnie's cup.

"One cup is enough."

"I'll take some." Damon reached over her shoulder with a cup in his hand and let Mickey pour him some coffee.

Marnie tensed at Damon's sudden appearance. *He moves as quietly as a cat,* she thought.

"That coffee smells good. I couldn't resist it. Nothing's better than fresh brewed coffee in the morning."

As Damon sat next to Marnie, she stood and asked, "Does anyone want some toast? I'm fixing a piece for myself and would be glad to add some for you all."

They both nodded. As Marnie reached for the bread

on the top shelf of a cabinet, the motion of the yacht slowed, then came to a complete halt.

Marnie stared at Damon with a question in her eyes. "Do you think . . . ?"

Damon leaped to his feet. "I hope . . ." Leaving his sentence unfinished, Damon hurried from the galley with Mickey and Marnie quickly following behind him.

When they stopped at the wheelhouse, where Canie lounged against the doorjamb chewing on the stem of his pipe, Marnie knew the sonar device had indicated the sunken ship might be under them from the beaming smile on the old man's face.

"I believe we found her," Canie said. "Let's check it out. Something's down there. And Don said the metal detector indicates that there are metal objects below us, too." Canie took the pipe out of his mouth and added, "This is what we have been waiting for. I can feel it in my bones."

"I hope this isn't another wild goose chase," Mickey said as he turned to head to the stern of the boat, where the diving equipment was stored.

Marnie grabbed Damon's arm. "May I go this time? I want to try out a new camera and take some shots underwater."

Damon looked at the hand she gripped his arm with, then at her. "Okay. I'll leave Mickey aboard."

She started to say, "Thank you," but Damon turned and strode away. Her brows knitted.

"He has a lot on his mind, little missy. If this is the ship, the real work has just begun for him." Canie stuck his unlit pipe back into his mouth and entered the wheelhouse.

Marnie walked to her cabin and dressed in her bathing suit. When she reappeared on deck, she saw the frown that narrowed Mickey's eyes.

"Let's go, Marnie. We don't have all day to stand

around and gawk," Damon said, and tossed her a mask and flippers.

Marnie donned her diving gear, then checked to make sure she had everything she needed. After she opened the valve on her tank, she thrust the camera into Mickey's hand.

"When I'm in the water, will you hand me this?" Marnie smiled, her eyes asking him to forgive her for taking his place.

He matched her smile, saying, "Sure."

"Are you ready?" Damon said.

Marnie nodded.

"Keep close to me. Remember, you haven't dived in deep water for a long time. You will have to ascend slowly, taking about fifteen or twenty minutes to decompress properly. Understand?"

"Yes, Damon. Let's go."

"If it's the wreckage, take as many pictures as you can in the time we have."

Making her way to the side of the yacht, Marnie sat with her back to the water, then plunged backward against the surface, landing in a sitting position. The water encased her in its warmth as she surfaced and tossed her hair behind her.

Marnie swam to the yacht and Mickey stretched over the side and handed her the camera. "You have about an hour and a half of air. The ocean floor is one hundred feet down."

She waved, then swam to where Damon and Toothless were treading water.

Damon submerged into the water followed by Toothless and Marnie. Marnie scanned the water, clear with bright shafts of sunshine streaming from the surface to touch the depths of the ocean floor. She felt like a bird flying in the sky as she glided almost effortlessly toward the bottom.

When Marnie neared the seafloor, she saw the skeleton of a half-buried ship on the bottom. Hope surged through her as they headed for the wreckage. Damon inspected the visible part of the hull and turned to give the signal that he thought they had found the ship. Elation replaced her hope as Marnie began to snap some pictures of the little that remained of the once magnificent Spanish galleon. She thought of this ship sailing the Atlantic Ocean proud and majestic and how now it was eroded by the salt water, covered by marine organisms and sand. *So humble,* flashed through Marnie's mind as she moved away to take a wide shot of the skeleton of the ship.

She paused to watch Toothless and Damon examining crevices and holes in the ship. She swam backward a few more feet and glanced down as her leg brushed a piece of fire coral. Pain shot through her as she jerked her leg away from the coral. Her eyes watered as she bit down on her mouthpiece. She gripped her camera, took several deep breaths, then managed to snap a few more pictures before she swam toward the pair.

She looked at her pressure gauge and noticed she only had a few more minutes on the bottom. *I can wait that long,* she told herself, but as the pain intensified she began to doubt she could wait. Her leg felt as if it was on fire, like flames licking at her flesh. She clenched her jaws together until she almost chewed her mouthpiece in two.

Toothless looked at her face, then down her body. He motioned to Damon, who followed Toothless's gesture with his eyes. Damon signaled to surface, then grasped Marnie's hand, and they started their ascent. Damon pulled Marnie toward the top, halting at ten feet to decompress.

When Marnie's head broke through the surface, she gripped at the bottom of the ladder and handed Mickey her camera. Her mind was consumed with the pain. She felt faint as Damon helped her up the ladder.

Collapsing on the deck, Marnie took in shallow gasps of air. When she looked at her leg, red and swollen, darkness swirled before her eyes. She wanted to surrender to the blackness that hovered over her, but Damon's tender voice touched her mind, and she focused on his words as he helped her with her diving gear.

"I'm going to take you to your cabin and take care of that leg," Damon said.

As he carried Marnie toward her cabin, she laid her head on his shoulder and closed her eyes. Damon cradled her closer to him as if he wanted to weld her slender frame to his dominant strength.

His soft voice floated through the velvet mist that filled Marnie's mind. "You'll be all right, Pet." His arms tightened around Marnie as the blackness engulfed her.

Chapter Eight

Pain sliced through her thoughts as her mind floated upward toward the light. Marnie whipped her head from side to side. A strong pair of hands restrained her as she started to bolt upright in bed, and her eyes flew open to stare into Damon's gray ones.

She raked her fingers through the wet tangles of her hair and tried to smile, a reassuring smile that she was fine, but her lips wouldn't obey the command. Instead she watched Damon inspect her leg, worry lining his face.

"That's a nasty scrape, Marnie. It's bad enough to brush up against regular coral, but fire coral is another matter. These waters off Grand Cayman are infested with it. You've had a bad allergic reaction to the poison, but I think you'll be fine in a day or two."

Marnie lifted her head and looked at her inflamed leg. It throbbed, making her grind her teeth together.

"I want you to take some aspirin. That should help

119

the pain," Damon said, taking her hand and squeezing it. "I know what you're going through. I once touched fire coral. It isn't pleasant, but it will stop hurting soon." Damon spread a paste over the inflamed area. "This meat tenderizer should help with the pain and healing. Fire coral is a protein-based poison, so this will help break down the poison."

"Thank you," Marnie mumbled.

"Try to get some rest." Damon rose and went into the bathroom and a few minutes later returned with a glass of water and aspirin.

After Marnie took the pills, Damon smiled, saying, "I'll look in on you later to see how you're doing," and then left the cabin.

Marnie listened to the distant voices up on deck, to the water as it lapped against the hull, and wished she was anywhere but in her cabin. Lying on her bed, she could think of nothing but the pain in her leg. Sleep evaded her as she heard the ticking of her travel clock, its loud sound vibrating through the cabin.

Struggling to sit up, Marnie mumbled, "I can't stay down here." When she placed her feet on the deck and stood, she had to clutch the bedside table for support until her legs felt stronger.

As she walked toward the stern, she tried to block the pain from her mind, but it worked its way into her thoughts. She clamped her jaws tightly together and forced herself to smile.

"How's everything going?" Marnie tried to make her voice sound cheerful, but it came out a little too shrill.

Toothless turned from filling a tank with air and asked, "How's your leg?"

Marnie waved her hand. "Oh, better. I'll be as good as new in a day or two."

"That's the fastest damn recovery I've ever seen," Toothless muttered, and resumed filling the tank.

"Where's Damon? Mickey?" Marnie eased herself into a lounge chair.

"They went back down for a few minutes to get another look at the wreck. Damon can't stay down there for long, so they'll be back soon. He'll have to bring in more divers in the next day or two. The water's too deep to work for long without having to decompress a lot," Canie answered.

"I've got some great shots of the part of the hull that's showing. There will be a lot of sand to remove to get to the lower decks, though." Marnie shifted in the chair to make her leg more comfortable.

"And that's what will take so long. Six months to a year, little missy."

When Marnie heard splashing, Canie turned from her. She raised herself with her arms and peered over the side of the yacht to see Damon and Mickey below, Mickey starting up the ladder.

When Damon clambered over the side of the yacht onto the deck, Canie asked, "Do you think it's the galleon, *Santa Santiago?*"

"I'm not sure, but it's a Spanish galleon. I hope we'll be able to identify the ship when we recover some of its cargo."

"Won't the name have been eroded from everything it was on?" Marnie asked.

Damon spun around and looked at her. "What are you doing up on deck? You should be resting."

"Mr. Wilson, I'm not an invalid. It only made it worse having to stay in my cabin and think of my leg as I lay staring at the ceiling. Now, surely the name of the ship won't still be stamped on anything."

"No, probably not, but the *Santa Santiago* was carrying a cargo of mercury for the mining of gold and silver in Mexico. If it's the ship, we may find some of the mercury still in her hold. I hope all of it."

"Why?" Marnie moved in the chair again, but the pain intensified as she changed positions.

"Because mercury is over three dollars a pound and that ship was carrying a hundred and seventy tons of it. That makes the cargo worth over a million dollars."

"I've already started spending my share of the profits," Mickey said as he took off his tank.

"Your share?" Marnie looked from Mickey to Damon.

"Mickey, Toothless, Canie, and yourself will share in the profits of this salvage. A million dollars will help you with that book you want to do on the Indians of the Southwest." Damon stepped closer to Marnie, his chiseled features noticeably softened.

"Carolyn didn't tell me I would share in the profits."

"I decided to make all the original members of the expedition partners." Damon unstrapped his tank and laid it on the deck.

"Then you aren't my employer anymore. I'm my own boss."

Damon twisted around to look at Marnie, his eyes gleaming. "Hardly. I still run this salvage and you'll still take orders from me. Now, young lady, I want you to go inside the aft cabin and at least sit inside where it's cool. It's going to be a hot day and you don't need to be out in the sun."

Marnie settled herself deeper into the lounge chair. "I don't need you to mother hen me, Damon Wilson. I'm perfectly capable of taking care of myself."

Damon's gaze traveled up the length of her, lingering momentarily at her breasts, then her mouth, before resting on her eyes. Before Marnie realized his intention, he bent over and swung her up into his powerful arms. "You're a stubborn woman, Marnie Stevens. Must I make you do everything?"

"And you're a bully. Put me down!"

Laughing, Damon said, "Don't tempt me to drop you on the deck here."

Marnie saw the mischief in his eyes. "You wouldn't with this leg of mine—would you?"

His expression became serious. "No, Marnie."

His voice sounded husky, deep. His hold tightened as he drew her toward him. Their lips touched for a moment as he leaned over and placed her on the couch. He slipped his arms from around her and pulled away. The color of his eyes turned smoky as he stared down at Marnie.

A lump formed in Marnie's throat, threatening to close it. She wanted to reach up and pull him back into her embrace, but her pride stopped her.

Turning away, he said, "Rest. I don't want to have to worry about you. I have a lot to do today."

Marnie found her voice, ragged from the emotions Damon stirred within her. "When will more divers be coming?"

"I hope in the next two days. I already contacted three of them while I was in Grand Cayman yesterday."

"Are you flying to Grand Cayman soon?"

"Yes, tomorrow. And when I get back I want to see you feeling better." Damon crossed the cabin and left.

She looked at the closed door for a long moment, releasing her pent-up breath slowly. The feel of Damon's lips on hers was engraved in her thoughts as she leaned back and closed her eyes.

Marnie watched the motorboat fade from her view, the image of Damon etched in her mind—his black hair tousled by the wind, his tanned arm raised in a good-bye salute. As she turned from the railing, she caught Mickey staring at her and smiled, then walked toward him, limping slightly.

"Is your leg better today?" Mickey asked.

"Much. With aspirin it doesn't hurt like yesterday. Thank goodness for that. If nothing else, I learned to be very careful when diving."

Mickey fell in next to her and walked with her to the salon. She sank into a chair and stretched her legs out in front of her.

"Are you and Toothless going down today?" Marnie asked, studying Mickey, who was sitting across from her.

"Yes, do you want to go down with us?"

"Do you think I should with this leg?" Marnie laced her fingers together and rested her chin on them as she leaned forward, her elbows propped up on the arms of the chair.

"I don't see why not—unless you think Damon would get upset."

Marnie remembered his last words to her: "Take it easy today. See you tonight."

"He might not like it, but then what he doesn't know won't hurt him. When are you going down?"

Mickey grinned. "I'm not responsible for your actions. When the boss finds out, you'll have to do all the explaining. Be ready in thirty minutes. I'm going to check the equipment out before we dive."

"I'll be ready, Mickey," Marnie called out to him as he left the cabin.

Marnie walked to her cabin, dressed in her two-piece orange bathing suit, picked up her camera, and headed for the stern of the boat. She watched Mickey and Toothless check the equipment and air pressure in the tanks, and when they were through Toothless handed her her diving gear. After donning her wet suit, then buckling her weight belt around her waist, she strapped her knife to her leg.

"I didn't get to finish taking the pictures I wanted to yesterday. This will give me a chance to get some shots before they start salvaging," Marnie said as she finished putting on her diving gear and made her way to the side of the yacht.

When she hit the water and surfaced, Mickey gave her the camera, then entered the water, too. They duck-dived to the bottom.

Again Marnie felt the sense of freedom envelop her, the sense of weightlessness exhilarate her. It was as if she were a butterfly gliding through the air, suspended over an alien world of beautiful shapes and objects that dazzled the mind.

Following Mickey and Toothless, she swam toward the sunken galleon, stopping once to take a picture of the ship. When she examined a thick piece of timber that was exposed on the seafloor, she thought of what it would be like to be on a galleon heading for the New World hundreds of years ago. She remembered the time a hurricane had struck where she had lived in Florida and the fear that had consumed her, a girl of fourteen. *What did those people on the ship think when the hurricane hit them?* she wondered, and tried to imagine what it would have been like. A shudder rippled through her.

Marnie moved around the wreckage to snap pictures of it from different angles. When thirty minutes had passed, she looked around in search of Mickey and Toothless and saw them inspecting something on the ocean floor. Swimming toward them, she noticed a huge crusted object sticking up from the sand, half buried in it. *A cannon,* she thought, and took a picture.

Suddenly the hairs on the neck stood straight up. As she scanned her surroundings, she became paralyzed with fear. Two sharks moved toward them like two menacing-looking machines. Nudging Mickey, she pointed toward the sharks.

Don't panic, bolted through her mind, but she had a

hard time fighting the panic that began to rise within her. *Stay still. They won't hurt you.*

Marnie slanted a look at Toothless and Mickey, who had both removed their shark sticks from their belts. They watched, too, as she stared at the sharks, now circling, eyeing the three of them.

Breathe normally. Don't hold your breath. Stay calm. Instructions filtered through her mind as she moved closer to Mickey, touching the knife on her leg.

One of the sharks came within a foot of Toothless. He struck it across its nose and it darted away. The other shark took one last look and followed its companion.

Relief flooded Marnie's senses. Mickey indicated to surface and she nodded her agreement. On the slow ascent she thought of the sharks and wondered where they were. She kept looking around her, waiting for them to reappear in the distance. When she surfaced, she quickly swam to the side of the yacht and scrambled out of the water.

Panting, she collapsed on the deck and took deep breaths to still the pounding of her heart. "Boy, that was close!"

"They were just curious," Mickey said. "But I wish they would be curious a little farther away than a foot."

"What happened?" Canie asked as he helped Marnie take off her tank.

"Two sharks were investigating our presence," Toothless answered.

"Nothing to worry about, little missy. There hasn't been a person in the islands killed by a shark or for that matter even attacked since I've lived here. They were harmless." Canie laid her tank on the deck.

"Tell that to my nerves. I don't think they have quit shaking yet. I'd prefer those harmless creatures swimming somewhere else." Marnie dried herself off, then wrapped her hair in the towel. "Anyone for a game of gin rummy?" She looked straight at Mickey. "Do you want a chance at winning your money back?"

"Oh, what a dame! You can't settle for a share in the million dollars you'll get when we recover the mercury. You want my money, too. Okay, I'm a glutton for punishment."

"I'm going to develop these pictures, then we can have lunch while I thrash you at cards. I'll even fix lunch for you all."

"You are weakening, Marnie. Before long I'll be able to beat you at cards." Mickey chuckled.

"We'll just see about that, Mickey Edwards."

Marnie laid down her hand and said, "Gin rummy. Now let me see how many points are in your hand." She counted the points as Mickey's pout deepened, then wrote sixty on the pad and placed her pencil by the paper. "There. That makes seven hundred forty points. Mmm. That's a grand total of seven dollars and forty cents. At this rate I'll be a rich woman in fifty years."

"I think I'd better stick to diving and leave the card sharking to you. I'm starved. That lunch you fixed us was good, but hardly enough to keep a growing boy like me in shape. Who's fixing dinner tonight?"

"I think Canie."

"Oh, no. I hope he can think of something better than tuna casserole for dinner."

"Well, if you don't like my cooking, young man, you can fix all the meals from now on." Canie leaned against the door with a smile threatening to break up his grim features. "I came to tell you that dinner is served. Come, Marnie. It'll be a pleasure to escort you into the dining room." Canie held his arm out for

Marnie as he threw Mickey a disdainful glance over his shoulder and added, "As far as I'm concerned, you're all the company I need at the table, Marnie."

Marnie sat between Mickey and Canie with Toothless across from her. After dishing up the beef stew, she broke off a piece of French bread, then tasted the stew.

"It's good," Marnie said.

"Well, since it's edible, I'll try it then." Mickey brought the fork to his mouth and eyed the stew before he ate it. "Not bad for a change. I think you've found something you can cook, Canie," Mickey shouted over the noise of the air compressor.

Canie scowled at Mickey. "I hope Damon brings back some fresh meat and vegetables. That freezer doesn't hold much."

"When he does arrive, don't say anything about me going down diving today. He might not like it. Especially if he heard about the sharks." Marnie glanced from Toothless, who smiled, to Canie.

"Sure. I won't say anything to Damon. I'll pass the word along to the other crew members not to, either. Damon can get mighty angry when someone doesn't do what he wants." Canie scratched the back of his head.

"You're right there, Canie."

Marnie sat paralyzed at the sound of Damon's voice slashing through the silence. Gulping down a mouthful of stew, she slowly turned to look at Damon. He sent her a smile that didn't reach his cold gray eyes. She thought of a storm when she looked at his face. A shiver moved along her spine and she studied her plate as Damon sat next to Toothless, a tense silence filling the room. The color drained from her face when she heard Damon's next words.

"So, Marnie, you dived today." His words held the frost of winter in them.

She met his gaze with defiance. "Yes, I did." She

tilted her chin in determination. "My leg feels much better. And besides, nothing happened."

"I'd say an encounter with sharks is something, wouldn't you?" Damon's gaze trapped hers, his eyes diamond hard as they drilled into hers.

"It was nothing that should concern you, Damon. Two sharks wanted to check us out, that's all." Marnie pushed her chair back and rose. "If you all will excuse me . . ." As she strode from the cabin, she still felt Damon's piercing stare, a shaft of coldness ripping through her.

When she stepped outside on the deck and felt the warmth of the breeze, she rubbed her arms and relished the fragrance of the night air. Looking up, she found the moon, a silver crest hanging in the darkness of the sky. She saw a star and closed her eyes to make a wish.

"Please let me walk away from this in one piece," she whispered to herself.

"Marnie."

She tensed.

"Why are you always fighting me? What if something had happened down there like yesterday?" Damon asked, placing his hands on her shoulders.

She whirled to face him. "What if it had? It wasn't as if I dived alone. Mickey and Toothless were right there and had everything under control. I'm a big girl. My leg was better this morning and I wanted to see the wreck to take some more pictures. You should see the shots I got. They're good ones, Damon."

"I told you once before that you were a stubborn woman. Stubborn may be too gentle a word to use for you."

Damon's eyes sparked with his desire as he started to lean forward.

Backing away, she brushed her hair from her face

and said, "Please, don't, Damon. It doesn't mean anything to you."

Damon seized her chin and forced her to look at him. "Can you now read my thoughts?"

He framed her face with his hands and kissed her. When she started to melt toward him, she screamed silently, *No!* As his lips began their gentle assault on her senses, she tore away and moved back until her legs pressed into the railing.

"I will not become one of your conquests, Damon. I won't!" She shouted the last sentence at him before turning and running to her cabin.

Chapter Nine

The sun's rays danced on the surface of the emerald-colored water as a light breeze cloaked Marnie in its warmth. She took a deep breath of the perfumed air, then exhaled slowly.

"I can't believe today is Thanksgiving and New York is having a snowstorm. That makes me appreciate being here even more. I'll hate going home next week." Marnie trailed her hand along the railing of the balcony as she walked toward the French doors that led into the living room.

Following Marnie into Damon's house, Mickey said, "I'm leaving the salvage in a couple of days for my two weeks off. But I'm ready. Toothless and I own a dive shop here on Grand Cayman and we need to attend to it from time to time. Personally I would like to just spend my time diving and lying on the beach. This shop wasn't my idea, but I guess I'll give it a try."

"I was just about to call you two. Mrs. Carson has

dinner ready." Damon stood in the doorway to the dining room, studying them.

"Thanks for asking me, Damon. I haven't had a turkey dinner in several years. Somehow on Grand Cayman I always let Thanksgiving slip by," Mickey said, and pulled Marnie's chair out for her.

"Since you two were the only other Americans on the salvage, I thought you'd enjoy the dinner." Damon was looking at Marnie, the tempered steel of his eyes softening but his raw male vitality strongly evident.

"It makes me feel homesick, but at the same time I don't want to leave Grand Cayman and return to the hustle and bustle of New York," Marnie said, acutely aware of Damon looking at her.

Mrs. Carson entered with a tray of tossed green salads, followed by dish after dish of food: a stuffed turkey, dumplings, snow peas smothered in a butter sauce, oyster dressing, and cranberry sauce.

Halfway through the meal Marnie collapsed in her chair, her arms hanging limply at her sides. "I can't eat another bite. Where do you two find the room to stuff all this food?" She examined her half-empty plate, then Damon's and Mickey's. "I don't believe you two could possibly leave this table without the help of a crane. You both are starting on your third helpings!"

"Boy, does this meal bring back fond memories," Mickey said as he spooned some more dressing onto his plate.

Marnie pushed her plate away. "Well, I'm the only smart one here. I'm going to save room for the dessert. You can watch me while I enjoy the pumpkin pie, savoring each mouth watering bite."

"Speaking of water," Mickey said.

"We were?" Marnie interrupted with a chuckle.

Mickey sent her a "be quiet" look, then turned back

to Damon and continued, "It won't be long before the first deck is completely revealed. Are you going to come back to the yacht with us this evening? I believe we'll be finished with the work tomorrow afternoon. Of course, that is, if we don't run into any unforeseen difficulties."

"I won't be able to come back to the boat until late tomorrow morning, but I plan on being there when we start on the second level. The artifacts we have found so far, after only three weeks of salvaging, are terrific." Damon sipped his wine, watching the effect his words had on Marnie.

"That cannon is a beauty. And the gold cross with the fifteen diamonds and pearls is a work of art," Marnie said. "Where it was found makes me believe its owner was on deck when the ship went down, clutching it in his or her hand, praying. I wonder who owned it?"

"That we probably will never know, Marnie," Damon answered. "That's the sad part of the salvage. We'll never know what really happened to the people as they traveled to the New World, their hopes and dreams. Or what happened the fateful night the storm hit them."

A strange silence permeated the room until Mrs. Carson entered with the dessert. Marnie was relieved to see her smiling face.

Mrs. Carson held the tray out for everyone's inspection. "The very American dessert of pumpkin pie with whipped cream." She placed the pie on the table and sliced pieces for them. After she spooned the whipped cream on top of each slice, she handed the first plate to Marnie, then one each to Mickey and Damon.

Mickey quickly ate the pie, then rose. "As much as I wish I could stay and lounge around to allow this meal to settle, I must go to the shop for a few hours before we head back to the yacht. Thanks again, Damon, for the dinner. See you later, Marnie."

When Marnie heard the front door close, she said, "I don't think I'll be able to move from this chair for at least an hour."

"I thought we would go sailing, find a nice quiet place along the beach, and snorkel. But if you want to sit here all afternoon while the beautiful day slips away, go ahead."

"Sailing! I haven't been sailing since I lived in Florida. When do we leave?"

"Now, if you can lift yourself from your seat."

Marnie bounced out of the chair. "Give me ten minutes to change into something a little more suitable than this sun dress." She swept her hand down the strapless canary yellow dress before she spun around and hurried up the stairs to the bedroom she used when she was staying there.

"Thank goodness I brought a bathing suit along," she whispered as she undressed and wiggled into the one-piece black suit with bold red and blue stripes diagonally across the front.

When she reappeared downstairs, Damon took Marnie's hand. "I think what I appreciate most about you is that I don't spend my time waiting for you. My time is valuable and I hate women who think it's fun to keep a man waiting for the hell of it."

"Where's your sailboat?"

"On the beach. I had James put it in the water this morning. I haven't had a chance to use it in quite some time. I hope I remember how to handle it."

Damon descended the path to the beach with Marnie right behind him, his hand still tightly clasping hers. Excitement tingled along her spine.

After Damon pushed the sailboat into the water, he held it in place for Marnie to climb in, then clambered into the boat and adjusted the sails to catch the light breeze.

"I hope you have oars just in case the wind dies down. I'd hate to get stranded out in the middle of the sea when night falls."

With mock indignation Damon pointed to the two oars in the bottom of the boat. "Do you think I'd come unprepared, Pet? My male ego is wounded."

"I doubt that could ever happen. You have too hard a wall around it." Marnie shielded her eyes from the glare of the sun and watched Damon guide the sailboat across the North Sound to a white sandy stretch of beach. When he had tied the sailboat to a palm tree, he pulled out a basket from a hidden compartment in the boat.

"Not a picnic lunch! Haven't you had enough food today, Damon?"

He laughed. "I always come prepared with a little refreshment." He stuck his hand into the basket and pulled a bottle of red wine out for Marnie to see. "A very good year."

"And what are we supposed to drink it from? The bottle?"

He held his hand up, palm outward. "Just a minute." Fumbling around in the basket again, Damon came up with two crystal wineglasses. "I think of everything."

"All the comforts of home." Suddenly Marnie was very hot, the cool of the water inviting. "Where are the fins and masks? You promised me we would go snorkeling."

"And that we shall do." Walking back to the sailboat, he removed snorkels, masks, and two pairs of flippers.

At the water's edge they sat and spat into their masks. Marnie dipped her mask into the water, sloshed it around, then dumped the salt water out. After she

135

placed the mask on her face, she pulled the straps over her head, then dipped her flippers into the water and put them on.

She stood next to Damon and asked, "Which way?"

"Out there." He pointed to the left.

He took her hand and they splashed out to knee-high water before beginning to swim. As Marnie hovered over the shallow reef, a school of yellow tail snappers swam by, one daring to come within inches of her arm. The multicolored parade of fish dazzled Marnie. A black and gray fish that looked like he was wearing a tuxedo darted into a hole in the coral reef. Marnie duck-dived to the bottom to get a closer look. When she surfaced, she blew water from her snorkel, then took a gulp of air. She swallowed some salt water that was still in the snorkel and choked. The salt water seared her throat, her eyes burning from the taste as she floundered in the water, trying to catch a decent breath that didn't gag her.

She trod water and spat the mouthpiece out. As the burning sensation subsided, she noticed Damon next to her.

"Are you all right?" he asked.

Marnie opened her mouth to speak, but no words would form in her throat, so she just nodded.

Damon pointed toward shore and they began to swim toward it. Marnie was exhausted, her legs and arms like lead. As she stretched her arms toward shore in long even strokes, she forced her legs to kick. When she reached the shallow water, she sank to the sand and took deep breaths.

Marnie sat in the shallow water for a moment and took off her fins, then stood, burying her toes in the sand. The waves pounded against her legs as she squeezed the water from her long blond hair. Catching the towel Damon threw her, she walked toward him.

"I think I could use a nice tall glass of ice water." Marnie rubbed her neck and swallowed to coat her raw throat.

"The first time I dived under the water with my snorkel I forgot to blow out and took in a mouthful of salt water. You don't have to do that twice to remember to blow out. It can really burn going down."

Marnie dropped down on the blanket that Damon had spread on the sand. "I thought I had cleared my snorkel completely."

"Thank God I was there to save you from drowning."

"I wasn't drowning." With her chin raised, Marnie sat straight, a look of dignity on her face. "I was merely gasping for air."

"Oh, I see." Damon suppressed a laugh and worked the cork out of the wine bottle. "Sorry this isn't water, but it might help."

Marnie took the wineglass from Damon and gulped the wine down. "Mmm. That does help. May I have some more?"

Damon slanted a glance at Marnie. "With much more of this wine, it won't be long before you'll fall into my clutches, fair maiden."

"So you had sinister motives for bringing me here to this secluded spot."

"I do have a reason for bringing you here other than snorkeling." Again Damon reached into the basket and brought out a wrapped present. "This is for you."

Staring at Damon, she exclaimed, "Why? It's not my birthday."

"Because I wanted to give it to you. Can't a friend give a friend a gift without a reason?"

Through a sweep of black lashes, she studied him. "Perhaps, Damon. I'm not sure." Slowly she unwrapped the gift, gasping when she saw the present.

"Damon! They are exquisite, but I can't accept them. They're too expensive." The diamond earrings glittered in the sunlight.

"Not for me. I want you to have them."

Marnie lifted the diamond earrings from the case they were in. "I've never had anything like them. They must be worth a king's ransom. Thank you, Damon, for thinking of me. But I must refuse." Sighing, she placed the earrings back into their velvet case and thrust the present into his hands.

He inched closer to her. "It's very rude to refuse a gift. I didn't hurt your feelings by turning down your present." He laid the case in her lap, then brushed his finger across her cheek. "Did I?"

"No, but . . ."

"Remember, I don't accept no for an answer." His lips were only an inch from Marnie's mouth, his breath caressing her. She breathed deeply of his male scent as his lips touched hers, claiming them in a long kiss.

He gently pushed her back until he lay beside her on the blanket. His hand moved down to massage her stomach in a slow circle as she wound her arms about his neck and pressed closer to him.

His lips left her mouth to trail kisses to her neck. He paused at the hollow at the base of her throat and teased her with his tongue. Her hold tightened on him, a wild, shaky excitement tingling along her inner thighs. Her flesh felt like it was on fire as her heart began to gallop.

He pulled back and stared down at her. As Damon stroked her cheek, he whispered, "I want you, Marnie. I have for a long time."

She smiled, her mind swimming in the sweet sensations that he had evoked. She drew him to her to whisper against his ear, "I love you, Damon."

He tensed, his hand halting its slow, sensual movement. He pulled away to sit a ways from her, bringing up his knees to rest his arms on them. He stared at the water, the silence lengthening between them.

Marnie's heart stopped beating for a brief moment. She pushed herself up to a sitting position and placed her hand on his shoulder.

"Marnie, I want you to become my mistress. Don't go to New York next week. Stay here on Grand Cayman with me at the villa. You were made for making love to. Your lips are so soft. Your hair is a silken gold." He remained with his back to her, looking at the water.

Marnie's hand slipped to the blanket, his words bombarding her. *I want you to become my mistress.*

No thoughts filtered through the hurt that sliced into her mind. She stared at his rigid back and fought to control the tears that spilled from her eyes. *Mistress! No!* She clenched her hands, numbed by his words.

Marnie slowly released her fists and stood. Her breathing became shallow, labored, then grew into a hissing sound that exploded from her lips.

"No!" Her heart was now frantically pumping the blood through her body. Marnie clasped her cold hands together until her knuckles turned white. "I won't be your mistress! Ever!"

When he rose and turned, a thin-lipped smile curled his mouth, his gaze moving over her slowly, a guarded look in his eyes.

Tears tumbled down her cheeks. Through a shimmering mist she watched him advance toward her. She dashed the tears away. "You're a conceited, arrogant . . ."

He gripped her arm. "I'm what, my dear?"

She yanked her arm from his grasp, her breast heaving from her fury. Her bitterness spilled over into her voice as she said, "You play with people for your amusement, not caring that someone will get hurt by your little games. Well, don't you worry about me. I'll get over this little infatuation *soon*. I'm just glad I found out what kind of man you are before it was too late." She whirled and faced the water. "I want to leave now. Take me to the airport. I'd rather wait there for Mickey than at your house."

"Suit yourself."

Damon gathered up the blanket and picnic basket, then brushed past her to throw everything into the sailboat. She stood immobile for a minute as he untied the boat.

"Well, I thought you wanted to leave *now*," he shouted.

Her legs moved automatically as she placed one foot in front of the other, the pain he had caused driven deeper into her mind.

As the wind screamed at her, Marnie sat in the bow of the boat and stared at the water. *It's your own fault, Marnie Stevens,* she told herself. *You knew he wasn't capable of loving anyone, caring about them. He doesn't know how. But you thought you could make things different for him. That was your mistake—thinking your kisses meant more to him than they did, that your love could change him.*

Marnie's mind burned from the memory of his kisses as they possessed her body and soul. She clamped her lips together to imprison a sob. *Why did I have to fall in love with him, then be foolish enough to tell him?* she asked herself.

But Marnie knew the answer as she remembered the streaks of pleasure that flashed through her when he had touched her. *All reason leaves my mind when I'm around him,* she thought.

When they reached the beach at his villa, Marnie

scrambled from the boat and walked across the rocky beach to the path that led up to his house. On the wide, open beach she felt as if she would suffocate from everything crashing in on her.

I must get away from him, collect my senses before I make a bigger fool of myself and accept his offer, she told herself, her vision blurred by tears.

She could see herself in his arms, his lips nibbling her flesh, his hands sending rivers of passion flooding through her. *No, I could never be his mistress, to be discarded when he was through with me. What kind of life would that be for me?*

"Marnie." Damon spoke her name softly, as if he were caressing it. His hand touched her arm, his fingers feather light along her flesh, the action halting Marnie on the path. As his hand traveled down her arm to her wrist, she stiffened.

"Marnie, my offer still stands. Stay with me." His fingers curled around her wrist and he spun her around to face him. "You like me to kiss you like this."

His lips teased the corners of her mouth, shivers shooting down her spine. Her legs felt like water as his kiss deepened and she leaned into his strength.

He whispered against her hair, his voice muffled by it, "You want to stay, Marnie. Your body wants me to touch it, to kiss it. You're fighting yourself and me." He stroked the small of her back as if he were a musician tuning his instrument.

She felt herself moving closer and closer, the word *Yes* on the tip of her tongue. She quivered from the need of him, her body a tightly strung violin waiting to be played—by him.

"And when we part you'll be a rich woman. Those earrings are only the beginning of the gifts I'll shower on you, Pet."

"No." The word was wrenched from her very soul as she stumbled backward, staring at him. "You can't buy me. I'm not for sale, Damon."

"Everyone has a price, Marnie."

"Then mine is too high for you. I want marriage, a man to love me for a lifetime. Can you afford that price?"

As she flung the question at him, she turned and hurried up the path, not waiting for his answer. *I don't have to wait,* she thought. *I could see the answer in his eyes.*

When she reached the top of the cliff, she scanned the front of the house and saw James washing Damon's Mercedes by the garage at the side of the villa. She ran across the drive, glancing back to see if Damon was behind her, her heart thumping so loudly that she was sure James heard it.

The tall, slender man with salt-and-pepper hair straightened and looked down at her. "Yes, ma'am. Can I be of help, Miss Stevens?"

"Yes, I'd like to be taken to Mickey Edwards's dive shop. Do you know where it is? Will you drive me there?"

James stared at her for a moment, indecision in his hazel eyes. He looked over her shoulder, a question now in their depths.

"Drive her wherever she wants to go, James." Damon stood a few feet from them, his face impassive as his cold gaze flicked over Marnie. "I'll be in the house when you get back." He turned and walked toward the front door to the villa.

James placed the drying towel by the hose, rolled down his sleeves, and opened the door for Marnie. When she climbed into the Mercedes and rested her head on the back cushion, she closed her eyes.

Damon dominated her thoughts in the darkness. She

tried to concentrate on what she would do when she returned to New York, but with each image she saw Damon. Her eyes snapped open and she tried to focus on the scenery. But all she saw was a blur of greens and blues as her eyes burned with her unshed tears.

When the Mercedes stopped in front of Mickey's dive shop, Marnie mumbled, "Thanks," and scurried from the car before James had opened his door.

Mickey was standing behind the counter talking with a customer, when Marnie entered the shop, the threatening tears beginning to stream down her cheeks.

Mickey looked up and hurried to her. He guided her into the office at the back of the shop and placed her in a chair. "I'll be right back, Marnie."

When Mickey reappeared, Marnie had managed to control her crying. She sniffed and rubbed her nose with a tissue that Mickey had handed her.

Reclining against his desk, he folded his arms across his chest. "Tell me what happened, Marnie."

A lump formed in her throat, making it impossible to say anything. In a choked voice she finally whispered, "Damon—Damon and I fought." She tilted her head to look into his soft eyes and saw concern and friendship in their depths. "I love him and all he wanted me to be was his mistress! I couldn't do it, Mickey. I want to be near him but not that way. I have to have more than a man's crumbs." A tear fell from her cheek onto her hand. "What am I to do? It hurts so much."

Mickey knelt in front of Marnie and cradled her to him. "I know, Marnie. Time will heal the wound. I had thought perhaps this once it would be different for Damon. You're special. Maybe he'll come to his senses soon and see what he's letting slip through his fingers. Damon isn't a fool—at least not until now."

"But how will I be able to work on the salvage with Damon there? I don't think I can do it."

"You'll be going back to New York next week. That will help. You're strong minded and able to do anything you set your mind to. Who knows what will happen in the future? Don't worry about it until the moment occurs."

Pulling away, she rose. "You're right. He won't be on the yacht much in the next week. I can avoid him. Then when I'm in New York, I'll see Carolyn about getting out of my contract."

"But this is too important to your career. Think about that. You have done some beautiful work already. You deserve all the credit."

Marnie shook her head. "I know my limits. I couldn't come back here every month and be near him and not touch him, kiss him. No, I have to get out of that contract."

Chapter Ten

Marnie froze. She squinted and watched the motorboat heading for the yacht. As it sped closer, she turned and strode from the aft deck into the cabin and moved to her quarters below deck. When she closed the door to her cabin, she rested her forehead on the cool wood.

Stay calm, she told herself. *You knew he would return.*

She straightened and inhaled deep breaths of air to steady her hammering heartbeat. It was as if the strength in her legs had flowed from them until nothing was left to support her. Numb, she sank onto the bed and stared at the door.

"You can't avoid him, Marnie," she whispered.

The sound of the motorboat bumping the hull of the yacht crashed in on her thoughts. She could imagine Damon climbing aboard, his presence felt by every member of the crew as he walked along the deck, inspecting what had been done while he was gone. She thought of him fingering an artifact that they had found earlier that day—a beautiful gold jewelry box with a delicate lacework pattern on its lid.

Marnie sighed and consciously arranged her features into a neutral expression. *I can do it,* she thought. *I can face him.* But the dull throbbing ache of her heart made her words sound hollow.

She rose. *I have a job to do,* she reminded herself. *He's my employer. And that's all.* She pinched her cheeks to add some color to her pale features. *Just remember. Only my employer.* With a quick glance at the pair of cream-colored shorts and tank top she wore, Marnie raised her chin, determination in her stiff stance.

As she started for the door, she heard a light tap. Mickey coming to warn me, she thought, and opened the door.

When Marnie saw who stood in the passageway, her body grew tense, but she strove to keep her expression calm. "What are you doing here, Anita?"

"Well, aren't you going to invite me in?" Anita pushed past Marnie into the cabin, inspected the quarters in a swift appraisal, then turned and continued, "Not bad. I prefer Damon's villa, though. That's where I'll be staying for the next week rather than on the boat. I just came over to see what this salvage was all about while Damon checked on the progress. I heard about the beautiful pieces of jewelry you all found."

"Anita, I'm busy. I don't have time to sit and chat." Marnie started to leave, a numbness encasing her. Her breathing tore from her lips as she fought for a decent breath.

"I won't keep you long. I just wanted to see how you

were doing." Anita walked to the door and stood next to Marnie. "Damon's so kind and considerate. Even though he'll be here most of the day, he's going to travel back to the villa at night to be with me." Anita formed one of her pouts that made her look very sexy. "So I won't be alone in that *large* house of his. You know how frightened I get about being by myself. Say, I might even visit the yacht on some of those days when he'll be here. We could . . ."

Marnie didn't hear the rest of what Anita was saying, because her gaze was drawn to the diamond earrings in Anita's ears. *The ones Damon gave to me. The ones I left on the beach.*

Nausea boiled in Marnie's stomach as she focused on what Anita was saying, clenching her jaws together until pain shot down her neck.

"I'm so glad you introduced us, Marnie. He's so rich. And did you know he owns television stations, magazines, and newspapers? He's already arranged for a modeling job for me with one of his magazines, *The World of Fashion*. That's one of the biggest magazines in the country! It might have taken me a long time to get a job with them, but overnight I am to model for a spring issue."

Marnie moved out into the passageway, trying to keep the sick feeling from rising into her throat. Perspiration beaded her brow as she walked away from her stepsister, but Anita followed her.

Halfway down the passageway Marnie whirled and faced Anita. Marnie whispered, "He'll use you for a while, then throw you away. If that's what you want, then good luck, Anita."

Anita's golden eyes became pinpoints. "I know where I stand with Damon. I'll use him to get that break I need, and if I can make him fall in love with me,

147

that's even better. Just think of all the wealth and power that he commands. It's exciting just to be around that man."

Marnie turned to leave.

"You couldn't be jealous because he wants me and not you?" Anita shook her head. "No, Damon isn't your type. You two are too different. I enjoy the presents he gives me. You would rather slave away trying to make a living with your camera. You're a fool."

Marnie glanced over her shoulder at Anita. "I'll live my life the way I want. You are the one who'll be hurt in the long run." Her voice was so low it was almost soundless.

Marnie hurried up the ladder to the aft cabin and made her way outside to the bow of the boat. The muscles in her stomach knotted as she leaned against the railing and stared at the cool water that seemed to call to her. It lapped against the hull, water splashing up, then falling back into the sea to be whisked away to some faraway place. She bent farther over the railing, wanting to cup her hands in the water and cool her flamed cheeks.

"Marnie." Mickey's soft voice was full of concern.

She pulled back and faced him.

"Are you all right, Marnie?"

She offered him a faint smile that faded almost instantly. "No, Mickey. Do you know that he flew to New York and brought my stepsister down to stay with him for the next week? Why? I don't understand. I'm confused."

Mickey stepped closer, drew her into the circle of his arms, and stroked her back, trying to force the tenseness from her.

Against his shirt she said, "I don't think I'll be able to make it through the next few days, Mickey."

"I'll be here if you need me, but the sooner you face him, the easier it'll be. Don't avoid it for long. The dread of it will turn you into a bag of nerves."

Marnie listened to the even pounding of his heartbeat and drew strength from it. The knot in her stomach began to loosen.

"Mickey, don't you have some work to do? I believe you're to go down next."

At the sound of Damon's voice her stomach constricted again, but her mouth set in a stubborn line.

"I'll be all right, Mickey," she whispered, then looked into the coldness in Damon's eyes.

"And don't you have some work to do, Marnie?" Damon asked.

"Yes, as a matter of fact, I do." She succeeded in keeping her voice steady, even though she quivered with all her warring emotions at the sight of Damon standing so close. He was dressed in tight-fitting jeans and a shirt that hugged his body, revealing his muscular chest.

She started to walk past him when she heard him say, "Did Anita find you? She was looking for you a while back."

She halted, her body stiff, then turned slowly. "Yes, Anita found me." She made her voice sound so sweet that it dripped with honey.

"I'm glad. She hadn't heard from you and was worried."

Marnie let her gaze move over him with all her bitterness within it before she pivoted. "I'm sure she was concerned. Now, I must get to work." There was a metallic ring to her voice.

Marnie heard Anita's soft laugh roll from her throat and glanced over her shoulder to see her stepsister standing beside Damon. His frown disappeared as he looked at Marnie a brief moment before turning his attention to Anita. He smiled down at Anita and said something to her. Marnie looked away and quickened her pace, the image of Damon and Anita together imprinted in her mind forever.

"Are you ready to go inside, Marnie? You know we can always turn around and leave," Mickey said, taking her arm and guiding her nearer the front door to Damon's villa.

"Don't you see I have to go to this party? I'm a part of the salvage and expected to attend this gala. I can't let Anita think her presence here on Grand Cayman disturbs me any more than I have already shown. And I have to show Damon—save some self-respect. Besides, with all those people he's invited tonight, I'm sure I can avoid Damon and Anita." Marnie forced a smile to her lips, but inside she felt the pain of her decision to come to the party.

"Well, at least tomorrow you'll be heading back to New York until the New Year. Maybe getting away will help, even though I'll miss seeing your pretty little face."

She stopped and turned to look at Mickey. "I won't be coming back here. I'm not a masochist. I know what it would be like being around Damon all the time. I couldn't do that. This will be our good-bye tonight, Mickey. But I hope you'll write every once in a while and let me know how things are going."

He shrugged. "You know me and work. I'm not good at writing anything, but for you I'll scratch a few notes on a piece of paper and send it to you."

Marnie stood on tiptoes and kissed Mickey lightly on the lips. When she moved away, she heard someone clearing his throat behind her and turned to see Damon standing in the doorway, a frown lining his face.

"I don't think you need to stand on my front drive

150

and make a spectacle of yourself. Come inside."
Damon turned sharply and entered his house.

Marnie and Mickey looked at each other, then at the
empty doorway. Finally Mickey said, "I guess we'd
better follow orders."

Marnie pasted a smile on her face and climbed the
steps. When they entered the entrance hall, she listened to the voices of the people in the living room for a
moment before she gathered her courage to walk into
the room. As she stepped into the living room, Marnie
scanned the group and saw Miles, Toothless, Canie,
and Phil, a new diver on the expedition. She smiled at
Canie and nodded toward Miles and Phil. Anita and
Damon were nowhere to be seen. Marnie relaxed some
of the tension in her and walked toward the bar.

"What would you like to drink, Marnie?" Mickey
asked.

"Nothing stronger than water. I need all my senses
intact tonight."

"Well, I haven't seen you in a while. How have you
been, Marnie?" Miles approached them, a drink in one
hand, a cigarette in the other, a crooked grin on his face
and his eyes twinkling.

Mickey handed Marnie her water and said, "I need
to talk with Toothless a minute."

Marnie smiled. "Tell Toothless hello for me." Then
she turned to Miles and asked, "Have you done any
swimming lately?"

"No, but I enjoyed a nice dinner here a few nights
ago in the company of your very delightful sister.
Charming, and a total waste on Damon."

"How nice." Marnie began to walk away from the
bar when she saw Anita and Damon coming through
the French doors leading to the balcony.

Damon looked straight at her, then placed his arm
around Anita's shoulder. Pain stabbed Marnie's heart

as she pulled her gaze away from him. *He wants to hurt me,* she thought. *Why is he being so deliberately cruel?*

"Ah, I see Anita now," Miles was saying, but Marnie ignored him, the pounding of her heart drowning out his voice. She gulped down the water, then set the glass on the bar.

Miles touched her arm. "You know, once I started to tell you about Catherine. Well, Anita looks a lot like her. No wonder Damon is attracted to her. He must have never gotten over Catherine."

Catherine and Anita look alike!

The walls were closing in on Marnie, the room's temperature now ten degrees hotter than only a minute before. *I can't stay here,* she thought, and looked around the room for a way to escape. She saw the doorway to the entrance hall was clear and headed in that direction. Slipping away from the party unobserved, she made her way upstairs to the room where she had stayed a month ago.

When she opened the door, the heavy scent of Anita's perfume enveloped her. She stepped into the room and noticed Anita's clothes flung over a chair, her shoes lying near the bed. Sinking into a chair, Marnie stared at the bed. Images of Damon and Anita teased her thoughts. Marnie rubbed her moist palms together, then buried her face in them. Names bombarded her mind—Catherine, Damon, Anita. The letters swirled in the darkness, mixing, coming together.

Marnie jerked her head up and felt herself breathing deeply. She felt like she was suffocating, as if she was breathing underwater and the regulator was shut off. Her breath came in gasps as she bolted to her feet and strode to the sliding glass door.

Marnie stood on the balcony and stared at the ocean. *You must get hold of yourself,* she thought. *Anita doesn't know how you really feel about Damon.*

Tossing her hair behind her shoulders, she tilted her head back to look at the diamond-studded heaven. *Damon's making it very clear how he feels about you. He doesn't want any permanent commitments and he's letting you know,* she told herself. *Go back to the party and act as if nothing is wrong.*

She had turned to leave when she caught sight of a light streaming onto the balcony from Damon's room and found herself being drawn toward the room.

Marnie tested the sliding glass door and it opened to her touch. Stepping into the room, she halted and released a slow whistle at the luxury of the bedroom.

A very masculine room spread before her with a king-size oak bed that drew a person's attention to it immediately. The bedroom was done in colors of navy and beige with two wingbacked chairs and a table near the floor-to-ceiling windows that ran the length of one wall.

She wanted to touch his personal things, but she stood rooted to the spot, staring first at a picture of an older woman on his chest, then at the disarray of clothes scattered on his bed.

"I don't remember inviting you to see my room."

Marnie spun around as her hand flew to her mouth to stifle a gasp.

"Have you decided to reconsider my offer to stay with me? Where's your luggage?" Damon looked around Marnie.

The color drained from her cheeks as she saw Damon's gaze make a slow sweep of her body. He took three strides toward her and stood inches from her. He touched a wisp of her hair, then traced a finger down her jawline.

"Perhaps you don't need any luggage." His voice was strangely husky.

For a brief moment Marnie felt trapped by the

intensity in his eyes, the soft words he spoke cascading over her. Then a blaze of anger surged to the surface of her dazed mind. She drew her hand back and slapped him across the cheek.

"Don't you think one woman at a time is enough?"

A myriad of emotions slipped across Damon's features with anger finally seizing him.

Marnie shrank back. She stepped away from him until she felt the bed press into her legs. A hard glint appeared in his steel-colored eyes as he advanced closer, taking each step slowly, his gaze locked with hers.

Marnie swallowed with difficulty. "Don't come any closer."

He laughed, the sound brittle, false. "What will you do? Scream? These walls are thick. Downstairs the music is playing, people are laughing, talking loudly. I doubt you would be heard." His words were like acid, eating away at her composure.

Marnie felt as if all the strength had been sapped from her. She sank onto the bed, clutching the bedspread in her hands. "Please leave me alone! Damon, I'm going home tomorrow. Let me go in peace. Haven't you done enough?"

Damon stepped forward, his hand reaching out to her. Then suddenly he pivoted, cursing beneath his breath, and stalked from the room.

Overcome by a fresh wound, Marnie stared at the glass door, the inky blackness of night beyond it. "Damon, why couldn't you have loved me?"

Her heart throbbed at a slow, painful pace as she grasped the bedpost and pulled herself to a standing position.

In a daze Marnie walked downstairs and through the foyer to the living room. She caught sight of Mickey and nodded at him. He spoke a few more words to Canie, then weaved his way through the crowd toward her.

"Do you want to go?" Mickey asked.

"Yes, take me to the hotel. I'm glad you were able to get me a reservation. I could never have stayed here."

"Let's go. Parties aren't for me anyway. I'd much rather escort a beautiful young lady around the island." Mickey placed an arm around her shoulder.

As Marnie started to leave, she felt eyes drilling into her back and glanced over her shoulder. Damon was staring at her, his eyes cold, his expression stony. She shuddered.

"I shouldn't have come, Mickey. It proved nothing."

A lump closed her throat, tears brimming her eyes. Marnie gritted her teeth. *I don't need him.*

She moved with the motions of a person in a trance as she walked from the house toward the car and climbed into it, everything a blur.

When Mickey pulled up in front of the Grand Caymanian Hotel, he turned and said, "I'll pick you up tomorrow morning in time for your flight. Do you want me to walk you to your room?"

Marnie turned and looked at him. For a moment she let the words sink in, then answered, "No, I'm fine. I'll be in New York tomorrow night. Things will be better then."

They have to be, she thought. *I can't have Damon, so I must learn to live without him.* But as her thoughts dwelled on Damon, her heart constricted.

Chapter Eleven

The train in the toy store window went around and around in circles. Marnie heard the Christmas music in the background, the Santa Claus ringing his bell. She shifted the weight of the packages in her arm and released a slow sigh. Turning from the brightly decorated window, she began her trek down the street toward her apartment building.

Marnie looked up at the gray overcast sky and knew it would snow before the night descended. *Maybe a warm cozy fire and a cup of hot chocolate will lift my spirits,* she said to herself, but Marnie knew it wouldn't. *Four more days until Christmas and I'm about as low as you can get. And this is supposed to be a happy time of year.*

Marnie thought about the cold, impersonal Christmas she would be spending in her apartment alone. *Why did Bill and Mom have to go to Europe this*

Christmas when I need them so much? she asked herself as she entered her apartment building.

She opened the door to her apartment, stepped inside, and tossed the packages onto the sofa before she collapsed next to them. She propped up her feet on the coffee table and kicked off her shoes, then wiggled her toes and flexed her feet. Slowly the numbness wore off and she rose to walk into the kitchen and put the water on to boil.

Through the kitchen doorway Marnie saw the pile of packages and thought of the presents she had bought for Mickey, Toothless, and Canie. "I hope they get them in time," she said aloud. She remembered the pipe she had mailed last week to Canie. "He should love that new pipe and tobacco." Smiling, she imagined the older man sticking the pipe into his mouth, unlit, and chewing on the stem.

I wish I could spend Christmas with them. With Mickey's cheerful voice and Canie's wild stories I would be able to forget Damon for a few hours, Marnie told herself, the water whistling in the kettle.

Marnie fixed herself a cup of hot chocolate and moved back into the living room. She opened a package and fingered a cuddly doll, a tightness threatening to close her throat.

"Amy should have those pictures by now," she whispered, her heart heavy with the knowledge that this would be Amy's last Christmas. "She'll like this doll. I'll send it tomorrow as a belated present." Marnie placed the doll back in its box and put the gift from her sight, the doll a reminder of Amy's condition.

Sipping the steaming brew, Marnie leaned back to rest her head on the sofa cushion. She scanned her small living area and thought about the mess that had cluttered the room only two weeks before. Memories of the long flight back to New York crowded her mind—watching Mickey wave to her at the airport, wishing Damon would arrive at the last minute and beg her to stay—forever.

Marnie straightened and placed her cup on the coffee table. *I don't need anyone—especially someone like Damon Wilson,* she thought. *I'll make it without him. I have up until now—but it will be the hardest thing I've ever done.*

When the doorbell rang, Marnie jumped. She stared a moment at the door before she rose and walked across the room toward it. She imagined Damon standing in the doorway with a smile on his face, his eyes sparkling with a silver gleam, but when she opened the door Carolyn stood in the hallway. Marnie stared at her agent for a moment, then fell into her arms.

"I'm so glad you're back from Maine, Carolyn. I've wanted to talk with you for two weeks. What a time to take a vacation!"

"From the look on your face a moment ago I wasn't the one you wanted to see standing here." Carolyn stepped back. "Well, aren't you going to invite me in, or are you going to tell me what happened on Grand Cayman out in the hallway?"

Marnie laughed for the first time in weeks. Seeing Carolyn made her feel better, as if part of her troubles would be over. "No. Please, come in and have some hot chocolate."

Carolyn removed her heavy overcoat and gloves. "I hope you'll serve me something better than that, or at least lace it with a generous portion of brandy."

"All I have is some red wine. Would you care for a glass?"

"Now that doesn't sound too bad. Fill it to the top. This first day back at work was murder and I need it." Carolyn flopped into a chair and took off her shoes.

"And to top it all off it's snowing outside. It just started. Oh, why did I have to go to Maine for two weeks? I should have gone to Grand Cayman and seen this salvage for myself."

Marnie moved into the kitchen, then minutes later reentered the living room with Carolyn's wine and placed it on the coffee table.

"Well, now how was the assignment? Tell me all about it. Was Damon Wilson a charming host? I hear he really can be. Did you enjoy diving? What have you all found on the wreck?" Carolyn shot the questions at Marnie in rapid fire.

Marnie held up her hand. "Hold it. One question at a time. The most important thing I have to tell you is that I want out of the contract I have with Damon. I can't go back to that island and work for him."

Carolyn pushed her hair back from her forehead. "I think that one request answers all my questions." She shook her head slowly. "I don't know if I can, Marnie. To be truthful, I thought you would only work for a few months, that that would be all he would need you for. But if he wants you longer, the contract stipulates he has top priority on your time until this salvage is completed."

"Find a way for me to get out of that contract." Marnie's voice rang with determination as she paced the floor.

"Let me see what I can do at the agency, since he's one of our clients. He might let you back out of your contract. We can try, Marnie. That's all I can promise now." Carolyn took a sip of her wine. "I hear he's in town for a few days. He's visiting his mother for Christmas."

Marnie halted her pacing. "He's in town?"

"Yes. I just missed him at the agency today."

Marnie's heartbeat accelerated. *Damon's here,* she

thought, and wiped her damp palms on her jeans. *What if I see him? What will I do?* She clenched and unclenched her hands. *You won't see him. New York is a big city.*

Marnie relaxed a little and sat across from Carolyn. "Tell me, how was your trip?"

"Boring. Why I keep going back to that small town I grew up in is beyond me. I'd much rather hear about Grand Cayman. Is it as beautiful as I've heard?"

"Oh, yes! The beaches are clean with fine white sand. The water is crystal clear with many different shades of blues and greens. And the people are so nice. The crew on the salvage was very friendly."

"Then what went wrong, Marnie?"

"Damon Wilson," Marnie murmured. "Remember when you advised me to be careful? Well, I wasn't. I fell in love with him and he didn't return the feeling."

"Oh, Marnie, you didn't!"

Marnie stared at the carpet. "I guess I'm guilty of falling under his spell." She looked up and met Carolyn's gaze. "And I'm paying dearly for it now. Do you know he wanted me to be his mistress? *His mistress! Me!*"

"Then he certainly doesn't know you very well, Marnie. I think you're one of the few virgins in New York over the age of twenty-three." Carolyn laughed, a deep throaty sound. "In this day and age a lot of men don't know how to handle a woman with those feelings. Robert is a fine example of that. He kept pressing you to go to bed with him and finally, after months of no, he got tired of trying—then Anita came along."

Marnie's fingernails dug into the arms of the chair. "I'd rather not talk about Anita."

Carolyn sighed. "What did she do now, Marnie?"

"She was with Damon on Grand Cayman."

"He'll tire of her soon. Men always do with women

160

like Anita. They like a challenge and she isn't one."
Carolyn rose. "I must be going. But I hope you'll come
over Christmas Eve. I'm having a few friends over for a
small party."

"I would love to. And after Christmas I'm going to
start on that project I always wanted to do."

"*If* I can break that contract, Marnie. Don't count on
it. You're probably one of the few women that has
rejected Damon Wilson. He might not be very charita-
ble."

After Marnie closed the door when Carolyn left, she
slumped against it. *He will just have to let me go,* she
thought. *Why is it always one extreme or the other with
that man where I'm concerned?* Her head began to
throb with the tension she felt. Marnie rubbed her
temples and pushed herself off the door, then walked
into the living room and sank into a chair.

Marnie stepped back to examine the small Christmas
tree with its red and gold balls. The branches hung
down from the weight of the ornaments and string of
blinking lights. "Well, at least it adds a little Christmas
cheer to this apartment," she said aloud.

She placed the few presents she had under the tree,
fingering the one from Mickey. Then she picked up the
small gift of Canie's, shook it, and tried to guess what
was in it. She started to open the present, then firmly
placed it with the others.

"You only have five presents to open on Christmas as
it is, Marnie Stevens," she chided herself. "Don't make
it four. Tomorrow will be soon enough."

The ringing of the phone brought Marnie around.
She hurried into the bedroom and answered it.

She stiffened. "What do you want, Robert?"

"May I see you today?"

"Robert, I'm busy."

"Perhaps I could come over tonight and wish you a Merry Christmas."

Marnie heard the pleading tone in his voice and weakened. "Carolyn's having a party tonight. I'm going, Robert."

"Good, then I'll take you. Carolyn invited me, too."

Marnie released a slow breath and said, "Well, okay, Robert. I'll be ready at eight."

"Thanks, Marnie." Robert hung up the phone, his voice heavy with emotion.

Marnie stared at the receiver for a moment before replacing it in its cradle. *Why does Robert want to see me now?* she wondered. *Well, I guess I'll just have to wait until tonight.* With a glance at her clock on the bedside table, she saw that it was six.

Now what am I going to do for the next two hours? she asked herself, and inspected her fingernails, which looked in need of a manicure. She was moving toward her dresser when the doorbell rang.

Halfway across the living room Marnie heard the lock on her door flip and halted, every muscle taut. She stared at the door as it swung open, then trembled with relief when Anita entered the apartment.

Marnie drew herself up to her full height. "Don't you believe in allowing someone time to answer the bell? I want that key you have. You no longer live here and don't need it."

Anita frowned. "Sure," she said, then tossed the key at Marnie, who caught it and pocketed it in her jeans.

"What do you want, Anita?"

"I came to see you and to bring you a present."

Marnie eyed the wrapped box in Anita's hand.

Anita thrust the gift at Marnie. "Here. Open it now if you like."

Marnie sat and opened the present. She lifted a

beautiful tortoiseshell comb out of the box and turned it over in her hand. "It's lovely, Anita. Thank you."

"I'm glad you like it. I know we've had our differences, but everything's going so great now that Damon has helped me get that big break I needed." Anita sat across from Marnie. "He took me to the turtle farm on Grand Cayman and I couldn't resist buying it for you. But I had to sneak it through customs. Even though it's made from farmed sea turtles, you can't bring it back into the States. Grand Cayman is . . ."

Marnie felt numb as Anita rattled on about the island. Marnie remembered her own trip to the farm with Damon as her guide, her heart twisting with pain. *Those times with Damon were special to me,* she thought. *Even my memories are ruined now.* Tears smarted her eyes, and she dropped her gaze to mask her expression as she half listened to Anita's babblings.

". . . the warm water. The best time I had, though, was sailing around to the North Sound and eating lunch in an isolated cove. What a romantic spot!"

Sailing to the North Sound! No!

Marnie stood, her arms stiff at her sides. "Thank you again for the gift, Anita. Now if you'll excuse me, I have a party to get ready for."

"Yes, I have to be running along, too. Damon's in town and we're going out. Merry Christmas." With those final words Anita strolled out of the apartment.

When the door closed, Marnie slowly walked back into the living room and noticed the tortoiseshell comb on the coffee table. She sank into a chair and stared at the gift. *What has happened to my life?* she asked herself. *Everything is all wrong. If only I hadn't met Damon. If only . . .*

From afar she heard the clock over the mantel chime seven times. Marnie straightened, strode to her bedroom, and slowly moved through the motions of getting dressed. She slipped a long black gown over her head and down her body. It clung to every curve as she zipped it up the back and smoothed the shiny material into place. She clasped a single strand of pearls around her neck, then put on black satin pumps and gathered up her black beaded purse.

As she made her way into the living room, the doorbell sounded. When she opened the door, her breath caught in her throat. Damon stood in the hallway dressed in a black tuxedo that fit his body perfectly.

"Why are you here?" was all she could manage to say.

"Because I need to see you," he answered, his voice harsh, crisp.

"I don't think we have anything more to talk about. Besides, I don't have the time to talk, Damon. I'm going out in a few minutes."

"What I have to say to you won't take longer than a few minutes." He stepped into the apartment.

As Marnie shut the door she saw the look of anger that creased his brow, the glint that shone in the depths of his eyes.

"Do you remember what I told you once about what I would do if you tried to back out of our contract, Marnie?" His question was spoken in a deadly quiet voice—too quiet.

Marnie moved forward to catch what he was saying. She swallowed to coat her suddenly dry throat. "Yes."

"And it still holds true. You work is unfinished and I'll not be forced by you to look for someone to finish what you have started."

The savagery that seemed to creep over his features left Marnie shaken, but she drew the last vestige of her courage together and glared at him. "Find someone else to finish your book. How can you expect me to work for you after . . ."

Ignoring her, Damon said, "They have cleared another deck. I want pictures of that deck after it's cleared and pictures of the artifacts. You started this project and you *will* finish it. I won't let you back out of it gracefully." His eyes were two narrow slits, his mouth a tight line set in grim determination.

Her gaze lowered beneath his icy blast. She stared beyond Damon, fighting the raging emotions within her. *I hate you, Damon Wilson.* Anger trembled through her to instantly recede into a numbing depression. *No, I love you. Why can't you love me? Why did I have to fall in love with the unattainable?*

"Okay, Damon, I'll report back to the yacht the third of January." She looked him in the eye. "Now, if you would leave so I can get ready for my date, I would appreciate it." She opened the door wide for him.

Damon stared at her for a long moment. It was as if time stood still as his gaze bore into her, seeking, probing. Her flesh burned where his eyes roamed. She felt the flames of rage in his eyes sear her skin as he moved forward and stood just inches from her.

Marnie smelled his masculine scent that seemed to always drug her senses and wanted to reach out to draw him to her, to run her fingers along his mouth, to feel the soft black curls of his hair. His breath mingled with hers. His unwavering look imprisoned her in a hypnotic trance.

He leaned closer, his lips grazing hers. "Don't be late, Marnie. If you aren't there on the third, I'll start working to carry out my threat." His voice was diamond hard, his words slashing out at her.

Marnie shrank back from the force of his threat. She

stared wide-eyed at him, the breath driven from her lungs. He smiled—such a cold smile that Marnie shivered from its impact. Then he turned to leave and stopped abruptly when he saw Robert in the hallway.

Damon's gaze raked over Robert, a frown still harrowing Damon's eyes. Without a word, Damon turned and walked away, but not before Marnie saw the savage look engraved in his features.

Marnie clasped her hands together to still their trembling as she watched Damon step into the elevator, the doors closing shut on his thunderous look.

Robert turned to look at her. "What was Damon Wilson doing here? I thought he was in Grand Cayman working on that salvage."

Marnie fought to keep her expression neutral, her voice level as she waved her hand. "Oh, he's visiting his mother for Christmas."

Robert walked past Marnie into the apartment and sat in a chair as if he had never been away from her—and Anita had never come between them. Marnie closed the front door and moved into the center of the living room. Her heart raced from the sudden encounter with Damon, a river of fire flowing through her veins.

"Would you care for a glass of wine before we go to Carolyn's party?" she asked. Slowly her heartbeat returned to its normal pace.

Robert looked at her, a warmth in his blue eyes. "Like we used to do before we went out? That would be nice. Those were good times, Marnie."

Marnie turned from the smoldering look in his eyes and walked into the kitchen. She filled two glasses with red wine, then made her way back into the living room.

After she handed him his glass, Marnie sat as far away from Robert as possible. She sipped her wine and watched him over the rim as he inspected the apartment.

Finally he blurted out, "I've missed seeing you, Marnie. I want to see you again."

Marnie gripped the glass for a moment before she loosened her hold and placed it on the table. "That's not possible, Robert. I feel nothing for you. The day I found you and Anita together on that couch was the day my feelings for you died."

Robert leaped to his feet. "I was wrong, Marnie. I knew it right away but didn't know how to get out of the mess I had made of things. Anita wasn't for me." He ran his fingers through his sandy blond hair. "Why I ever thought she was is beyond me." He moved his head from side to side, a puzzled look on his face.

Marnie rose. "I think we'd better go now. I don't want to be late for Carolyn's party. She says it's just a small get-together, but if I know her, there will be at least fifty people there."

Robert grabbed her arm and pulled her to him. "Please think over what I said to you about us."

"You're hurting me, Robert. Let me go." She yanked her arm from his grasp and rubbed her bruised flesh. "Don't say anything else to me about it or I'll go alone to the party."

"Okay, Marnie. Have it your way for the time being."

"Not just for the time being, Robert, but for always."

My world is upside down, she thought. *What am I going to do? How am I going to handle the salvage assignment?* All the way to Carolyn's apartment the questions plagued her until her temples protested with a pounding that spread down her neck to the muscles in her back.

When Carolyn opened the door to her apartment, still no answers came to Marnie. She pushed the questions to the back of her mind and entered the apartment. There was a surprised expression on Carolyn's face.

"What are you doing here with Robert? Are you seeing him again?" Carolyn whispered to Marnie.

"We just came together. Believe me, I have no intentions of starting that relationship again."

"Good. It would lead nowhere. I do have some bad news for you, though. Damon Wilson won't . . ."

"Let me out of my contract. I know. He paid me a visit just before the party to tell me personally." Marnie couldn't keep the bitterness from her voice.

"Well, I also have some more bad news."

"What could be worse, Carolyn?" Marnie's stomach muscles contracted as she watched a frown appear on Carolyn's face.

"Damon Wilson is here tonight with my boss—and Anita is with him."

Marnie grew taut.

"I didn't invite him, Marnie. My boss brought him along. What was I to do? Throw the man out—our best client?"

"Oh, heavens, no! No one should ever do anything to upset Mr. Wilson."

"Marnie, you didn't tell me you were coming to the party." Anita glided across the floor toward Marnie, a smile plastered on her face. "Damon will be glad to find out you're here. You two probably have a lot to talk about since you work so closely together. Damon!" she called out.

The sound volume in the room went down several levels as people stared at them, their conversations interrupted. Damon lifted his head and glanced toward

Anita. When he saw Marnie standing next to her, his mouth thinned into a tight-lipped smile. He crossed the room in four long strides and stood next to Anita.

"It's good to see you again, Marnie." His voice held no warmth in it, his smile dissolving into an impassive expression.

Before the lump in her throat grew and she made a fool of herself in front of everyone, Marnie turned from the couple and followed Carolyn into the living room. She felt Damon staring at her and fought to carry herself with pride and dignity, but her legs felt like jelly, her heart hammering so loudly she knew everyone in the room heard it.

Marnie grabbed a glass from a tray, gulped the champagne down, then replaced the empty glass and took another full glass before the maid walked away. She sipped the sparkling liquid, some of the depression lifting from her as she finished the second glass. Marnie walked to the bar and had her glass refilled. She felt her confidence build as she gripped the stem of her glass.

"Marnie, I didn't get a chance to tell you how beautiful you look tonight. I didn't appreciate you enough when we were dating," Robert said close to her ear.

"You're right there," she said. Marnie ran her tongue over her dried lips and took another drink.

"I hope you'll think about what I said to you earlier in your apartment. I mean to date you again. You're so much better than Anita."

"We are through, Robert. I cannot make it any plainer than that."

Marnie brushed past Robert and escaped onto the balcony. A cold wind ripped through her, but she ignored the icy chill and stepped closer to the edge to clench the iron railing. She leaned over it and watched the traffic moving along the street below, the people hurrying down the sidewalk. Then she looked up at the velvet sky, a thin crest of a moon suspended in it.

"So he's the Robert you spoke about that day at my house," Damon said, standing a few feet behind her.

Marnie tensed but didn't turn around. Instead she continued to inspect the star-studded sky.

"Have you decided not to talk to me, Marnie?"

She turned slowly. "What would you like to talk about, Mr. Wilson? The salvage?"

"I've been thinking. We have to work closely together for the next year, Marnie. I'm willing to overlook the incident about the contract. Don't you think that for the sake of the rest of the crew we should call a truce?" He covered the distance between them and wrapped his arms around her waist, drawing her close to him. Marnie breathed deeply of his male scent and relished the soft feel of his silk shirt next to her cheek. Then she remembered Anita, Damon's threats, and backed away.

"How thoughtful of you." She glared at him. "What are you trying to do to me? You have no heart, Damon. Only a machine that keeps your body running."

He held her hand in a viselike hold. "There's no room in the world of business for a heart. It's a cold, calculating world out there, where you need to think with your head, not your heart."

Marnie searched his stony features. "Then I feel sorry for you, Damon Wilson. You're living only half a life. If you let Catherine's betrayal rule the rest of your life, then she has won and you aren't the man I thought you were." She tore her hand from his bruising grip and fled the balcony.

Marnie found Robert and said, "I'm going home. You can stay, but I'm leaving."

He looked at her in an odd way and said, "No, I'll escort you home. Are you all right?"

Marnie watched Robert through a shimmering haze of tears. She clenched her teeth and brought her raging emotions under control. "I'm fine—no, I have a headache and want to leave. I'd rather you stay." She turned toward the door.

"I'll come with you." Robert retrieved their coats and whispered their regrets to Carolyn.

Marnie avoided the questioning look on her friend's face and stepped outside into the hallway. She allowed Robert to help her with her coat and to guide her to the elevator. Her head throbbed, her temples hammering against her skull. The muscles in her throat tightened. She swallowed with difficulty, and felt drained of all her emotions, her mind numb.

When they reached her apartment, Marnie let Robert insert the key and open the door. He moved inside and switched on the lights. Walking into the living room, she watched as Robert sat on the couch. A vision of Anita and him lying on that same couch leaped into her mind.

She shook the image from her thoughts and said, "I think you should go now. I'm tired and I really do have a headache."

Robert patted the seat next to him. "Come sit down and let me massage your neck. That'll help."

"No."

"You used to let me do that when you had had a rough day. Let me now."

Marnie shrugged. "Why not?" She sat next to him, his hands kneading the flesh of her neck and shoulders until some of the tension was worked from her.

"You know it's no use with Damon Wilson. Men like him are attracted to women like Anita."

171

The muscles in her neck tensed again.

His breath was a whisper on her neck. "I saw you and him on the balcony. He isn't the marrying kind, Marnie. You're wasting your time."

Marnie twisted her head around and looked at Robert, their mouths only inches apart. "At one time you told me that you weren't the marrying kind."

"I found out that I was wrong. Marry me, Marnie. I'd be good for you." His mouth brushed hers.

His kiss deepened, but Marnie felt none of the wild sparks of desire streaking through her that she had when Damon's lips had possessed hers. The numbness still shrouded her, making her stiff, unresponsive. Robert pulled away and stared at her.

"You're a fool, Marnie. He'll only break your heart."

I know, she thought. *He's already done that.* But aloud Marnie said, "And what do you think you did that night I found you with Anita? No, Robert, you're no better than Damon Wilson. Please leave now before I lose my temper and say something I would regret later." She stood and looked down at him, a frown on her face.

"Very well. But don't come crawling back to me." Robert rose and walked toward the door, stopping to look back at her. "You don't have a chance, Marnie," he said, then opened the door and left, the sound of the door slamming shut echoing in the stillness of the apartment.

Marnie fell back onto the couch and stared at the door. *I'll go to Grand Cayman and do my job. I can do it. Damon is just another man,* she told herself, but Marnie knew it wasn't true. Damon had ruined her chances of ever finding another man to love, to marry.

Chapter Twelve

Marnie descended the steps of the airplane and saw Mickey waving at her. Smiling, she waved back. He met her halfway across the landing strip and hugged her.

"It's good to see you again. Thank you for the shirt. I don't get very many gifts at Christmas and it's nice to be remembered by a friend," Mickey said.

"Thank you, Mickey. The perfume cheered me up on Christmas day."

"Damon told me to pick you up and make sure you get on the plane with me for Little Cayman. Are you ready?"

"As soon as I go through customs and you take me to see Amy in the hospital. Then I'll be ready to face the lion in his den."

"Give me your customs card and I'll get it taken care of. I have my connections," Mickey said, extending his hand for the information card.

Marnie waited while Mickey spoke with his friend and took care of everything. Then he whisked her out of the building to his convertible sports car and she got in beside him. Her long hair streamed out in back of her as they drove toward Georgetown, the warm breeze fanning her face.

When they reached the hospital, Marnie said, "I won't be long," then climbed out of the car and hurried into the building.

Amy was sitting up in bed when Marnie entered the room. The fragile-looking child beamed with a smile that made her whole face bright.

"Hello, Marnie. I'm so glad you've come to see me. I loved the pictures you sent me and that doll is one of my favorites. Damon looks so funny in his wet suit and tank." She giggled, a sound sweet to Marnie's ears.

Marnie sat on the edge of the bed and clasped the child's cold hands in hers.

"I couldn't leave for the boat without paying you a visit. You're a very special person to me."

"Damon came to see me yesterday. I missed him when he was in New York. I always miss him when he's away from the island." Amy leaned closer to Marnie and lowered her voice a level. "Do you know he told me that I might be the flower girl at his wedding soon?" She sank back on the pillows. "Damon is going to get married! I can't wait!"

Suddenly a look of horror appeared on the small girl's face as she brought her hand up to cover her mouth. "Oh, Marnie, I wasn't supposed to tell anyone. It was our secret. Please don't say anything to Damon or anyone. I think, though, he wouldn't mind me telling you, since you two are such good friends."

Marnie's heart skipped a beat, then began to pound against her chest. She was sure that Amy heard her heart hammering—the sound was deafening. Marnie closed her eyes for a second and tried to calm the racing of her pulse. *He's going to marry,* she thought. *Anita? Yes, it must be her.*

"Marnie?" The girl's voice broke into Marnie's thoughts.

Marnie focused on the worry in Amy's face and forced a smile to her lips. "Oh, I'm sorry. I was just thinking what a beautiful flower girl you'll make at his wedding. I've got to run now, but I'll be back soon." Marnie kissed Amy, then stood, her legs weak, her knees shaking.

Marnie made it to the car without collapsing, but when she saw Mickey's kind face, she felt her control slipping. Tears welled in her eyes.

"What happened?" Mickey asked, taking her hands in his.

"Amy told me that Damon plans on marrying soon. *To Anita!*" Tears rolled down Marnie's cheeks. Through the mist she saw the concern on Mickey's face. She took the handkerchief he handed her and patted her face dry. "It seems all I can do lately is cry. I keep telling myself he isn't worth it, but it doesn't matter. I still cry."

"When a person is in love, a lot of things don't make any sense. That's love for you." He cradled her to him and let her cry on his shoulder.

When Marnie finally composed herself, she looked up at him and said, "Somehow I will survive this week, but right now I don't know how I am going to do it."

"You're strong. You'll do it," he whispered.

Marnie stepped onto the yacht, and as she braced her legs apart to get used to the feel of the boat beneath her, she watched two divers surface and climb onto the yacht, each carrying a sack of artifacts. The boat bustled with activity, people working busily at their jobs.

It has begun, she thought, and moved toward the cabin assigned to her. She laid her suitcase on the bed and opened it, taking out her cream-colored shorts and a T-shirt. After dressing she made her way up onto the aft deck to see what had happened since she had been gone.

When she approached Canie, the old man brightened with a smile. "It's good to see you again." He chewed on the pipe she had given him for Christmas. "This is the best damn pipe I've ever had. You're a girl after my own heart. If I was thirty years younger, the men on this boat would have to beware of me."

She gave him a smile and then kissed his cheek. "You are all talk. I think you have already captured my heart."

"That would be just my luck. When I'm too old to do anything about it." He scratched his gray beard.

"Are there going to be any more dives today?" Marnie asked.

"No, but do you want to see some of the things that they have brought up in the last few days?"

"Yes, I would love to. Have they found anything unusual?"

"They found another gold cross with diamonds and rubies in it that is worth a small fortune. It's a work of art. The craftsman that made that cross spent a long time fashioning the delicate lacework pattern on it." Canie took her hand and pulled her along the deck. "Come, I'll show it to you—and the other things, too."

The table was laden with golden objects, two wine decanters, pieces of jewelry, coins, silver and pewter flatware, dice, and several bronze swivel guns were on the floor. Marnie fingered a silver medallion, then the gold cross that Canie had told her about. As she touched the jewels on the cross, she considered the skill it had taken to create it.

"Well, I'm glad you could make it," came a deep voice behind Marnie.

Marnie turned slowly and looked into Damon's gray eyes. Her heartbeat quickened as she stared at him standing in the doorway dressed only in his bathing suit, his hair damp. She watched his muscular chest expand with his breathing for a moment as she gathered her wits about her to speak.

"Hello, Damon," she said breathlessly.

"I'm happy to see you made the plane for Grand Cayman."

"Did you doubt me? You really didn't give me any choice." Suddenly Marnie wanted to hurt Damon as he had hurt her. "I don't like being forced into anything and every minute I'm here I'll wish I was back in New York. I hate being away from Robert, especially after we have patched up our differences."

Marnie straightened and walked past Damon out onto the deck, where the air wasn't electrified with his presence, where she could breathe better. She leaned against the railing and watched the sun set, the sky aflame, the water like molten lava.

"Have you seen Damon yet?" Mickey asked as he came to stand behind her.

She nodded, her gaze fixed on the crimson clouds that stretched to the horizon.

"Marnie, if you need me, I'll be here for you. My shoulder will always welcome your touch."

She twisted about to look at him and ran her fingers down his jaw to his chin. "Thank you, Mickey. I have cried the last time for him. It's over for me. I have my whole life before me and a lot of things to do. When I get back to New York I'm going to start living again."

But silently she added, *But I'll never love another man—not after Damon.*

"That's my girl. Let's go eat. I heard Canie has fixed a turtle stew that is passable for food."

"The sacrifices we have to make on this boat to get the job done." Marnie laughed as she tucked her arm through Mickey's.

Throughout the dinner Marnie forced gaiety into her voice as she talked with Canie and Mickey. When she finished her dinner, she leaned back in her chair and planted her hands on her waist. "That was delicious, Canie."

Canie pouted. "Well, don't sound so startled that I could cook something that tasted decent. I have mastered several dishes." He stood, his body rigid with his mock anger as he cleared the table.

Marnie sipped her water and asked, "Where's Toothless? I miss seeing him."

"These are his two weeks off. We thought it best if one of us was always at the dive shop. That way things don't seem to go wrong," Mickey answered.

Marnie shifted in her chair. She felt uncomfortable with Damon sitting at the head of the table, not saying a word the whole meal. Sensing his eyes on her, she fixed a smile on her face.

"Would you like to go for a walk around the deck before you turn in, Marnie?" Mickey rose and held out his hand for her.

Without looking toward Damon, Marnie knew he stood and was walking from the cabin. She took Mickey's hand and squeezed it. "Yes, Mickey. Thank you again for your support. I wouldn't have been able to sit here without you keeping the conversation going throughout dinner."

They walked along the deck, Marnie savoring the warmth of the night, the perfume of the sea breeze. In silence Marnie and Mickey circled the boat, then stood before the door that led down to the lower deck.

"It has been a long day. I need a good night's sleep if I'm going to dive tomorrow."

"Good night, Marnie. See you tomorrow."

Marnie went to her cabin, the moonlight streaking through the porthole above her bed, and undressed in the moonlight. After she donned her nightgown, she slipped between the sheets and rested her head on the pillow, but sleep eluded her as she tossed and turned most of the night.

Damon haunted her thoughts. She pictured him walking down the aisle with Anita on his arm, the minister just having pronounced them man and wife. She sat up in bed, sweat drenching her, her gown clinging to her.

"Leave me alone, Damon," she whispered to the silent room.

But when she leaned back and closed her eyes again, she imagined Anita in Damon's arms, his deep, husky voice murmuring words of love into her stepsister's ear. Marnie turned over and pounded the pillow. Finally as the sky lightened, she dozed.

When she woke with a start, she bolted up in bed. Memories of her dream inundated her mind. She draped her legs over the edge of the bunk and stood, then stepped across the cabin to the bathroom. Looking into the mirror, she flinched at the dark circles under her eyes, at the paleness of her features.

She tried to hide the circles with makeup, but she could still see them, a beacon proclaiming her sleepless night to the world. Dressing in her black bathing suit, she sighed and muttered, "I can't hide in my cabin all day. I'll just have to make the best of this situation."

In the galley she grabbed a quick glass of orange juice and a piece of toast before she headed to the stern of the yacht. When Damon saw her, his gaze skipped over her before he turned back to prepare the equipment for diving.

"May I go down with the first set of divers?" Marnie asked.

"I'll be diving with Phil and Harry. You can be my buddy," Damon answered in a clipped tone.

Marnie dressed in her wet suit and donned her diving gear, then sat on the edge of the yacht while Damon helped her with her tank. She tucked her chin under and tumbled over into the water, then surfaced and deflated her buoyancy compensator before heading for the bottom.

When she touched bottom, Marnie marveled at the work that had been done on the galleon. She took several shots before swimming toward the ship, where she wanted to explore the two decks that were above the sand. With a glance to her side she saw Damon not far from her, her heartbeat accelerating at the sight of him.

She swam through an opening in the side of the galleon and inspected the area before her. Light streamed through a hole in the ceiling of the cabin she was in. She snapped another picture and headed deeper into the interior of the ship. When darkness began to creep in around her, she turned to start back out the way she came and brushed up against a slab of wood. It fell forward. Before she realized what was happening, a plank of wood one foot thick came crashing down on her, pinning her under it. She tried to move her legs, but the plank wouldn't budge, her heartbeat racing as panic claimed her.

She took several deep breaths. *Stay calm. Panicking is the worst thing you can do,* she told herself.

When her heartbeat slowed, she looked at her pressure gauge and saw that she only had twenty-one hundred pounds of air left. *Not much time,* she thought.

When she saw Damon, she nearly collapsed with relief. He signaled her with the okay sign and she nodded. He examined the slab of wood that lay across her legs and tried to move it but nothing happened. A stream of blood clouded the water around her left leg. Her legs were numb. Staring at the plank of wood, she could see that a piece of metal had pierced her upper leg.

Damon shook her arm to get her attention and again asked her if she was okay. After she nodded, he looked at her gauge that now read two thousand pounds. He motioned that he would have to surface and get some more air for her and himself.

Marnie watched Damon swim away, trying desperately to keep her breathing even, but as images of sharks being drawn toward the smell of her blood danced before her, her heart fluttered. She breathed deeply, her gaze riveted on the opening through which Damon had disappeared.

Please hurry, Damon, she prayed silently.

She glanced at her gauge again, panic rising into her throat, threatening to suffocate her. *Only two hundred pounds! Stay calm!*

But her breathing came in short gasps and her legs began to throb as the numbness wore off. Blood still drifted upward, making the water murky around her. The darkness of the ship seemed to grow in Marnie's mind. She thought she saw something coming toward her. She tensed, waiting, holding her breath.

She nearly fainted when Damon swam toward her, carrying an extra tank, with Mickey following behind him with a crowbar in his hand.

Suddenly no air came from her mouthpiece. She sucked in but nothing came out. Yanking out her mouthpiece, she grabbed for the regulator on the tank Damon brought with him as he neared her and breathed deeply, filling her lungs with the precious air. Damon worked to remove her useless tank as Marnie continued to inhale and exhale air from the tank that lay at her side.

Mickey wedged the crowbar under the wood and pressed down. The wood moved, shifting a little on her legs. Mickey put all his weight behind the lever and the wood was lifted up a few inches from her. Damon put his hands under her arms and pulled her out from under the plank, then signaled her to swim next to him while he held her tank. They swam to an opening and exited the ghost ship to begin their ascent.

When they surfaced, Canie lifted Marnie onto the yacht, then bent immediately and inspected the deep gash in her left leg.

"Don't look good, little missy. You need to get to a doctor and have him look at it." Canie tied a cloth around the leg to stop the bleeding.

Marnie felt faint, her head light from the loss of blood and the fear that had possessed her. When Damon and Mickey climbed on board, Damon knelt next to Marnie.

Her heart missed a beat when she saw the look of anguish on his face. She opened her mouth to speak, but no words would come out.

Damon picked her up in his arms and said, "I'm taking you to the doctor," then carried her to the launch, making sure she was comfortable before he started the engine.

Marnie was too stunned to speak on the ride to Little Cayman, but instead watched Damon maneuver the boat toward the island, his features grim.

When he tied up the boat at the pier and moved to

help her from the motorboat, he finally said, "The doctor isn't too far from here."

After arriving at the doctor's house, Marnie was taken away from Damon. She wanted him to come with her, to hold her hand, but the last she saw of him he was standing in the entrance hall watching her leave with the doctor.

While the doctor cleaned the wound and dressed it, Marnie wondered about the funny expression on Damon's face when the doctor had led her into his examining room. She shrugged. *He's impossible to figure out,* she thought, and turned her attention to what the doctor was saying.

". . . don't get to practice too much, but then I'm retired. Every once in a while there's a diving accident or something else that keeps me in shape. Now, I'm going to give you a tetanus shot if you haven't had one recently."

Marnie shook her head.

After she received the shot, the doctor walked to the door. "I'll tell that young man who brought you in that he can see you now. You'll be fine in a couple of days."

When Damon stepped into the room, he cleared his throat and started to say something, then stopped, raking his hand through his hair. A war of emotions played across his features as he stared at Marnie.

"Damon . . ."

Damon took one step, then another toward her until he stood in front of her. Speechless, she sat up on the examining table and returned his intense look. Sweat beaded his brow, the veins in his neck throbbing.

Then he spoke. "I thought I had lost you." He crushed her to him and against her hair whispered, "I love you, Marnie. I don't know what I would have done if you had been killed. A part of me would have died

A TREASURE OF LOVE

with you—my heart that you claim I don't have. Can you hear it thumping madly against you?"

Marnie listened to the hammering of his heartbeat that matched her own heart's wild pace and nodded.

"I wanted to tell you last night that I love you, that I need you more than anything in this world, but you threw Robert up in my face. My pride took over and I couldn't speak the words in my heart." He tilted Marnie's face up to look at the love that was mirrored in his eyes.

He bent and kissed her, a soul-giving kiss that sealed his love for her. Her mind swirled with her happiness as she clung to him. His lips nibbled her earlobe.

"I've been a fool. When you told me off that night at Carolyn's party, I knew you spoke the truth. I knew that I had been fighting desperately to not love you and I had lost the battle." He pulled back. "Can you love me? Will you marry me? I know I'm not the easiest man to love, but I'll make you happy. I won't let Catherine win—not if I can have your love."

Tears misted her eyes. Laughing, she dashed them away. "I told myself I wouldn't cry anymore, but these aren't tears of sadness. Yes. Yes. To both questions. I have loved you for a long time. What took you so long, darling?"

He smiled, following the outline of her mouth with his fingers. "A few days ago I promised Amy a wedding where she could be a flower girl. Is that all right?"

"I can hardly wait."

He cradled her against his chest, and she relished the feel of his strong arms around her, the feel of his bare chest against her cheek.

"We'll be married right away. If we wait too long, I'll be hard pressed to keep my hands off you. These last few months that has been the hardest thing for me to do. I kept finding myself wanting to kiss you, to make love to you, but I kept telling myself that you weren't for me, that no woman was for long. I've always gone from one woman to the next, never caring to stay long with any of them until you."

A doubt crept into Marnie's mind. "Damon, why did you bring Anita down to the island? You must have known how much that would hurt me."

Damon stiffened. "I'm not very proud of that. I wanted to hurt you, to drive you from me. I was scared of any commitment, and when you told me how you felt about me, I couldn't handle it. So I tried to destroy that feeling you had for me. And I nearly did." He cupped her face in his hands and stared down at her. "But I could never make love to Anita. I tried, but it wouldn't work. She wasn't you. I kept her around with the promise of a modeling job."

"I saw her wearing the earrings you had given me!"

"Correction. The earrings I had tried to give you. I felt if she wore them and you saw them that that would be the end of us. My faith in love wasn't strong. I'm glad I was wrong, or you wouldn't be sitting here now in my arms. After I met you, no woman could arouse me but you. I tried, but my feelings were dead unless I was around you. I didn't like that feeling either. Please forgive me, Marnie." His lips brushed her mouth.

In response to his plea, she wound her arms about his neck and pressed her lips to his. "Only if you promise never again to use the threat of ending my career against me."

Damon laughed. "I'm all bark and no bite. Even when I was fighting the feelings that I had for you, I wanted you near me, only interested in me, not Mickey or Robert."

"As Mickey would say, love does strange things to people."

"You're the most important treasure I found on this salvage," Damon whispered against her mouth before he claimed her lips in another mind-shattering explosion.

6 brand new Silhouette Special Editions yours for 15 days–Free!

For the reader who wants more...more story...more detail and description...more realism...and more romance...in paperback originals, 1/3 longer than our regular Silhouette Romances. Love lingers longer in new Silhouette Special Editions. Love weaves an intricate, provocative path in a third more pages than you have just enjoyed. It is love as you have always wanted it to be—and more —intriguingly depicted by your favorite Silhouette authors in the inimitable Silhouette style.

15-Day Free Trial Offer

We will send you 6 new Silhouette Special Editions to keep for 15 days absolutely free! If you decide not to keep them, send them back to us, you pay nothing. But if you enjoy them as much as we think you will, keep them and pay the invoice enclosed with your trial shipment. You will then automatically become a member of the Special Edition Book Club and receive 6 more romances every month. There is no minimum number of books to buy and you can cancel at any time.

IT'S YOUR OWN SPECIAL TIME

Contemporary romances for today's women.
Each month, six very special love stories will be yours
from SILHOUETTE. Look for them wherever books are sold
or order now from the coupon below.

$1.50 each

Hampson	☐ 1 ☐ 4 ☐ 16 ☐ 27 ☐ 28 ☐ 52 ☐ 94	Browning	☐ 12 ☐ 38 ☐ 53 ☐ 73 ☐ 93
Stanford	☐ 6 ☐ 25 ☐ 35 ☐ 46 ☐ 58 ☐ 88	Michaels	☐ 15 ☐ 32 ☐ 61 ☐ 87
		John	☐ 17 ☐ 34 ☐ 57 ☐ 85
Hastings	☐ 13 ☐ 26	Beckman	☐ 8 ☐ 37 ☐ 54 ☐ 96
Vitek	☐ 33 ☐ 47 ☐ 84	Wisdom	☐ 49 ☐ 95
Wildman	☐ 29 ☐ 48	Halston	☐ 62 ☐ 83

☐ 5 Goforth	☐ 22 Stephens	☐ 50 Scott	☐ 81 Roberts
☐ 7 Lewis	☐ 23 Edwards	☐ 55 Ladame	☐ 82 Dailey
☐ 9 Wilson	☐ 24 Healy	☐ 56 Trent	☐ 86 Adams
☐ 10 Caine	☐ 30 Dixon	☐ 59 Vernon	☐ 89 James
☐ 11 Vernon	☐ 31 Halldorson	☐ 60 Hill	☐ 90 Major
☐ 14 Oliver	☐ 36 McKay	☐ 63 Brent	☐ 92 McKay
☐ 19 Thornton	☐ 39 Sinclair	☐ 71 Ripy	☐ 97 Clay
☐ 20 Fulford	☐ 43 Robb	☐ 76 Hardy	☐ 98 St. George
☐ 21 Richards	☐ 45 Carroll	☐ 78 Oliver	☐ 99 Camp

$1.75 each

Stanford	☐ 100 ☐ 112 ☐ 131	Hampson	☐ 108 ☐ 119 ☐ 128 ☐ 136 ☐ 147 ☐ 151 ☐ 155
Hardy	☐ 101 ☐ 130		
Cork	☐ 103 ☐ 148	Browning	☐ 113 ☐ 142
Vitek	☐ 104 ☐ 139 ☐ 157	Michaels	☐ 114 ☐ 146
Dailey	☐ 106 ☐ 118 ☐ 153	Beckman	☐ 124 ☐ 154
Bright	☐ 107 ☐ 125	Roberts	☐ 127 ☐ 143

Silhouette Desire
15-Day Trial Offer

A new romance series
that explores
contemporary relationships
in exciting detail

Four Silhouette Desire romances, free for 15 days!
We'll send you four new Silhouette Desire romances
to look over for 15 days, absolutely free! If you decide
not to keep the books, return them and owe nothing.

Four books a month, free home delivery. If you like
Silhouette Desire romances as much as we think you
will, keep them and return your payment with the
invoice. Then we will send you four new books every
month to preview, just as soon as they are published.
You pay only for the books you decide to keep, and
you never pay postage and handling.

Silhouette Romance

Coming next month from
Silhouette Romances

Logic Of The Heart by Dixie Browning

Emma was looking forward to seeing the romantic island of Hatteras, and meeting Dan Slater added to the magic. She could see herself slipping into his arms and falling under his spell. . . .

Devil's Bargain by Elaine Camp

Was Alexis being caught up in an evil scheme or was Drayce's renewed love for her genuine? Their once passionate marriage seemed too distant to recapture those lost moments of ecstasy. Yet suddenly Drayce made Alexis forget why escape was so important!

Flight To Romance by Tracy Sinclair

Jennifer was not going to refuse Kalim Al Kahira, when he asked her to return with him to Egypt. She told herself her career demanded that she go—until she realized that there was no way to refuse his dark, penetrating eyes.

In Name Only by Roxanne Jarrett

Jill traveled to Brazil to enter into an arranged marriage. She was determined not to be ruled by her new husband, but soon she found herself unable to deny the mad passions that filled her with desire.

Sweet Surrender by Donna Vitek

Suzanne's trip to Italy turned out to be anything but the quiet visit she anticipated. For once she met Jared Caine she felt compelled to compete for his attention and show him the depth and breadth of her love.

The Second Time by Janet Dailey

Dawn returned home to the Florida Keys to seek peace in the turquoise waters. But soon calm waters are turned into turbulent seas when passions are ignited by her old flame Slater MacBride.

READERS' COMMENTS ON SILHOUETTE ROMANCES:

"I would like to congratulate you on the most wonderful books I've had the pleasure of reading. They are a tremendous joy to those of us who have yet to meet the man of our dreams. From reading your books I quite truly believe that he will some-day appear before me like a prince!"

—L.L.*, Hollandale, MS

"Your books are great, wholesome fiction, always with an upbeat, happy ending. Thank you."

—M.D., Massena, NY

"My boyfriend always teases me about Silhouette Books. He asks me, how's my love life and natu-rally I say terrific, but I tell him that there is always room for a little more romance from Sil-houette."

—F.N., Ontario, Canada

"I would like to sincerely express my gratitude to you and your staff for bringing the pleasure of your publications to my attention. Your books are well written, mature and very contemporary."

—D.D., Staten Island, NY

*names available on request